Also by Chris Else:

Why Things Fall
Dreams of Pythagoras
Endangered Species

brainjoy

CHRIS ELSE

TANDEM PRESS

This book was completed with the help of
a grant from Creative New Zealand.

Brainjoy is a work of fiction. Any resemblance
between any character and any real person
is entirely coincidental.

First published in New Zealand in 1998 by
TANDEM PRESS
2 Rugby Road, Birkenhead, North Shore City,
New Zealand

Copyright © 1998 Chris Else

ISBN 1 877178 34 9

All rights reserved. No part of this publication may be reproduced,
stored in a retrieval system or transmitted in any form or by any means,
electronic, mechanical, photocopying, recording or otherwise without
prior written permission of the publishers.

Cover design by Seven
Book design and production by Graeme Leather
Printed and bound by Publishing Press Limited, Auckland

For Barbara

PART ONE

the queen of heaven

Cities. There are cities so powerful that you might never know how they end. I've heard of one, for example, where the inhabitants have lost all hope of the outside.

1

Slam Geri Skumbags!

Shuttle station graffiti

A wet night in August, jack. It was cold, with the southerly whipping up the harbour, thrumming round the glass towers along the Petone foreshore. A block inland Spit Wilson was standing on the damp scurry of Jackson Street, annoyed, self-conscious, but keeping cool. He was always cool. He'd done an hour already, looking for a droppo club in an alley off Kensington Avenue, had to meet a slink there, friend of his. Jank, her name was. But nothing in it, jack. No club, no alley. Nobody to tell him where the club was even if he asked them, even if they knew which one he wanted; hundreds of them tucked away in cellars, in warehouses, the low-comm dumps of downtown Hutt. So he was acid with all this droppo shit, jack, and no kidoda. Stuck here on the street and dressed up like a fudgehead, in droppo uniform: the tight black jeans, the white rubber ankle boots, the reefer jacket, black, and white gloves buttoned at the wrists. He'd been doing droppo for three weeks now, mostly because of Jank, and it felt like four weeks too long. A wristic bloody wonderland that left you standing here in a doorway, hiding out, so fuckin low, jack. Nothing to do but watch the ords and butchers pushing past, the traffic hissing though the wet. Just staring as the rain chopped down, the big drops flashing bright like jewels in the waves of neon. No chance now except to hang out in the crowd like a raggy's arse, and all the wristers with their noses in the air. Or cosy up to the other droppoes, the real droppoes, staring at him, dopey, cause his clothes were new and clean. Or just say stuff it, jack, and catch the shuttle back up river, home sweet home to the geries staring at the TV in the welfpark flat. Farter and Muddler. FAM. Another fuckin Saturday night.

He couldn't live like that. He wouldn't. Keep it cool, then. Seize the day. Because Spit was sixteen and slick with it. He knew his way around. Not too many scams could catch him blinking. And he had a rationale, too, a wherewithal to make it stick. He'd seen it once on a campus vid, the Anonymous Society of Proteans whose symbol was the viper, jack, whose underlying principle the uncreated power of the Vacuum. ASPs, they called them. Slam-down secret. Shit, so secret none of them knew who the others were. Their own law, own game. Rules? There are none. Freedom in the soul to take the suckies down. And all the ex-ASPs on the vid were coughing their scams and their disguises, all the ords they'd done all over. Making out they were sorry, hurt themselves as much as they hurt you; but, shit, jack, Spit could see the difference, where the game lay. Knew. He knew it.

Power.
In the Vacuum, jack.

Visualise the Whole
Attitude Success
Commitment the Goal
Urgent it Today
Unique the Secret Soul, and
Motivate the Way

So use it now, he told himself. So do something. What? Well, anything. A random thing. Your destiny will seek you out. Like the place he was standing, the doorway to a bar. A big deal scam in here? He doubted it but maybe he could con a beer and have a game of Street Kings if he wanted. Even droppoes drank beer and they were nuts over the Kings. A noise to his left, the howl of a siren; the bulls were onto something, some poor luckout tagged in the biz. And hearing that made up his mind, jack. He knew the drill.

A flight of narrow steps behind him going down, blue neon sign above the door. Racers, it said. As good a dump as any. Inside and under was a narrow room, a bar along one wall with a row of stools in front of it. And dark as shit down here. The brightest light was the flickering TV screen up in the far corner. Banjax game. Two butchers, like coloured lizards, chasing each other round the rink. One was in lime green with white stripes, the other all electric blue. The flash of orange rollerblades. Spit had gone off that turbo stuff and he knew the droppoes hated it. He sat down on a stool near the door where the mez of the screen wouldn't get to him.

"Hey! Fuckhead!" Voice called out of the gloom. Was that for him? Well, shit, jack. Had to play it cool, though. Maybe scam a donny from a scene like this.

Three duds sitting up at the bar, hunched forwards with their forearms walling off their glasses and their eyes fixed on the screen in the corner. Video in slo-mo. He remembered that game. It was a classic play from the World Champs a couple of years back. Red Wallace with the drop on Mojo.

"What you want, son?" Barman coming towards him. Short dud, bald, with a thick neck smoothing down into his sloping shoulders. White shirt, crooked black bow-tie. His eyes were big and dark and his lips too, black looking in the low light, like they were painted on.

"Hey, er..." Spit looking vague, helpless droppy eyes.

"Don't give freebies," the barman said.

"Just a beer." Like a droppy droppo.

"I told you, creep."

"Yo, monster!" the voice down the room called, and another one gave a hoot of laughter.

"And I hate droppoes," the barman went on.

Spit gave up. Who gave a shit? "Not a droppo, not me," he said, squaring his shoulders in the reefer jacket.

"No? What are you, then?"

"Nothing. A nobody." Said it with certainty now, like he was proud of it.

"Don't serve nobodies either. Nothing don't pay."

Another hoot.

"Ssh!" A second voice, watching the game, although there was no commentary to interrupt.

The barman was staring at him, waiting.

"You got a Kings node?" Spit asked, looking for leverage in a new subject.

"Street Kings? You play that shit?"

"Sometimes," Spit admitted.

"You heard of the White Rabbit?"

"Sure." Like that was a dumb joke, no kidoda. Like everybody'd heard of the Rabbit, the undisputed champion of the video games network. He (or, maybe, she) had never lost a fight, they said, a winner of a million dollars plus, taking on duds from all over. Retired, now, the Rabbit. But even suckies knew about the dud.

"You ever play him?" the barman asked.

"No."

"Well, consider you're playing him now."

"Bouncy! Bouncy! Bouncy!" The voice down the bar gave the Rabbit's legendary cry of victory.

"So this rabbit don't give freebies to no droppoes. Okay?"

"I'm not a droppo. I'm..." he went looking for a word "... a spit." It was the only thing that came into his head and, shit, jack, what a dumb-arse thing to say. But it felt good, too, like a spit was a fine notion, a whole new thing. He was himself.

"A spit? What's that when it's counting its balls?"

"Nothing. We roam around. We cruise. First into one thing, then another."

"Sounds like a cockroach."

Spit staring at the bartender's face, the dark eyes, the black lips. The dud's mouth hardly seemed to move when he talked. Like his smile muscles were paralysed. A mean butcher, fuck sure. So who cared about one donny more or less?

"Beer," he said, giving up on it.

"And what's your name, spit?"

Spit hesitated.

"I said, 'What's your name?' You know the law."

Trapped now. Couldn't say he was Spit, could he? Spit, the spit? It made no sense.

"Arlen," he said. He had to say it, shithole name the geries gave him. He wasn't that, he wasn't, no way, not even pretending.

"Arlen? Ah!" The black lips opened a fraction to show an even blacker hole like the opening of a drain. "You got a card, Arlen?"

Spit pulled off his right hand glove and fished in his inside jacket pocket for his welfid card. The barman was already waving it away.

"I don't want your fuckin' life story, son. Just so I know you've got one. We'll call this a cash transaction."

From his side pocket, then, a five-dollar piece. Spit dropped it on the bar where it spun in a bright, shifting circle, ringing to a stop.

"Beer," the barman said. "Now you just remember, I asked you how old you was and you said eighteen and I asked if you was from this borough and you said yes. Got that?"

"Sure."

"And I asked you if you wanted to use the card and you said you'd rather pay cash."

"Yer, that's right."

The beer came in a tall glass with an inch of white foam oozing over the rim.

"And we ain't got no Kings node. This is a decent bar. People come here to meet each other, talk. Polite fuckin' conversation, okay?"

Spit said nothing. Sipped the beer and looked at the three dollars fifteen in change that lay on the counter. His last clink in the world until the next welfare credit. Maybe he should find a place with a Kings node, lever up his change a few bucks, little by little, ripping off the punks at the low end for ten cents a fight. But there was no fun in that, not any more. Making like some earnest-arse and counting it, like it mattered. ASP or spit, it made no difference, you had to treat the clink with *touch*, jack. Toss it like you had it easy, like a gold bar butcher. Attitude was all there was. And three dollars fifteen was at least another beer and the shuttle ticket back to Naenae.

"Good evening!"

A shift beside him, dark. A dud was climbing onto the next stool. And this one was a real wrist merchant dressed in a suit, jack, white shirt, bow tie. He was tall and thin with a round head and a long, pointed nose, and hair cut straight and blond and slicked down flat across his skull. His jacket and pants were made so narrow that his arms and legs stuck out like sticks, like jointed rods, like one of those flamingo birds as he sat down on the stool sideways, facing Spit, one elbow on the bar, one foot on the rail, his head tilted to the side and grinning. Freako sort of grin, jack, like a big loop in his face, and bright, staring eyes. So where did he jump from quick like that? Outside? No. He had a glass in his hand.

"Don't mind our friend, the monster," the dud said. "He has a colourful disposition, that's all. Part of the charm of the place." His eyes seemed to glisten in the dark.

"That's okay. It's normal."

"Ah, you understand these things. You've been around. And a round is not square, right? Not just a local neighbourhood bunny?"

"I cruise."

"Yes, yes. I heard you use that word before. What does it mean, exactly? Mmm?" A little twitch of his head, pulling back, bright eyes blinking. The light from the TV gleamed down the ridge of his bony nose.

"I guess..." Spit took a sip of his beer and thought about it. Play it cool. This dud had clink on him, maybe something a sly could get his fingers on. "I guess it just means take your chances, flip the coin, see which end comes up, jack."

"Is that how you happened to select this particular establishment? Taking your chances? Flipping your coin?"

"I guess."

"Your flip's not a flop, I hope."

A comedian, jack, a joke twister.

"The city," the dud said, "that's what interests me. The heart of the city. Know what I mean?"

A real wristic wonder, this one.

"Sure," Spit said.

"You know what this city runs on? What fires its belly?"

"Clink."

"Money? Oh, goodness me, no! No, not at all! Fear's what runs it. Plain unadulterated terror. You with me?"

Spit didn't answer. Didn't like the trend of all this much.

The thin dud lifted his hand and picked at his teeth with the nail of a bony forefinger. Then he took a sip at his drink. "Arlen the Spit, am I right?"

"Yes." He was stuck with it now in case the barman heard him otherwise.

"Tell me, Arlen the Spit, how would you like an adventure?"

"Adventure? What is this, jack?"

"Well, not really an adventure, that's an exaggeration. A job. That's more like it. Gainful employment. How would you like to do a job for me?"

"What sort of job?"

"Delivery." The dud reached into his pocket and pulled out a little package, a four centimetre cube, which he put down on the bar. It was wrapped in tissue paper, neatly folded with the edges taped down.

"What's in it?" Spit demanded.

"Nothing. Nothing of significance. Well, not quite true. It's of no monetary value and it's not a proscribed substance. Its importance is entirely symbolic. A present, shall we say? Or a sign, a meaning waiting for interpretation."

Spit stared at the package. He didn't like the thought of running errands, kids stuff, big kidoda. Still, at a price, maybe.

"What's the deal?" he asked.

The dud reached out a finger and slowly turned the package over to the left, then again, towards him.

"Campbell Terrace," he said. "Between Richmond Street and Scholes Lane. Are you familiar with it?"

"Sure." It was a couple of blocks away.

"You stand on the corner of Alley Two North and wait and when someone comes up to you, you say 'Tobin?' and if he answers yes, you say 'Blyss sent me' and you give him the package. Got that?"

"Yes." It seemed like nothing. *If* he did it. "What's in it for me?" he asked.

"Ah, well, now. For a person of your undoubted talent..." The dud smiled and suddenly his hand flipped from the package to Spit's change. Three dollars and fifteen cents disappeared under the long, thin palm.

"Hey, shit, jack!" Spit protested.

"No, no, no. Don't worry. Just a little test of your reactions, that's all." But the fingers didn't move. "I'll give you ten dollars for the job."

"Twenty."

"All right. Fifteen. You can have it when you get back. And you can leave your..." He lifted his hand and peered at the coins. "...your savings here, as a security. Just in case you decide to run off with my package. Fair enough?" He scooped the money into the side pocket of his jacket.

No, Spit wanted to say, no way. The deal's a heave, a whore slink heave. But then the dud was reaching out to him, patting his arm with a gentle, reassuring gesture, adjusting his lapels, and smoothing down his collar. The big, looping smile creased his cheeks and crinkled up into the crow's feet beside his eyes. And Spit felt a sudden knowing, knew it well that, shit, this was a nasty butcher, someone that didn't give you a whole heap of choice. You had no fuckin choice whatsoever.

"SKB," he said. "SK fuckin' B."

"And what does that mean?"

"Sha-Ka-Bla to you, jack."

"Absolutely!" the dud laughed like he knew it all. "There's a smart little spit, no? I'll give you twenty dollars if you're back in fifteen minutes. Okay?"

No, it wasn't okay but shit... Spit looked at his watch. Ten thirty. "Okay," he said.
"Good. 'Tobin', right?"
"'Blyss sent me'."
"That's it, Arlen the Spit. That's exactly it."

It was raining still and the wind was slashing it down into the north-side pavement. Spit at a run to the corner of Richmond, sprinted a diagonal, the four lanes of traffic, dodging the taxis and the freecars as he went. The east side of Richmond didn't look too good, though. Nobody around except a bunch of street jackers up ahead of him, gliding slow on their roller blades. They were moving away but they were still too close. Just so one of them would turn around and see a solitary droppo behind them, come on back like quick flash. He'd seen it happen. The turbs laughing as they jacked the droppo into pulp by the roadside. DTM, jack. Done to Mush.

He ducked into an alley to his left, a slot between two office blocks. It was a no choice, narrow and dark, and narrower and darker still towards the centre. Out ahead, he could see the yellow sodium lights on Scholes Lane. He took a few steps, rubber boots sloshed in the puddles, clinging heaps of damp garbage. He could hear the water gurgling in the drains. Not so good, he thought. Not so good. The problem here was some fuckin nonno bum with a blade. Or the bulls. If the bulls tagged him, it was a loitering charge for sure, and once they had him in, well, nobody got out of there but they were fitted up for something. And maybe the jackers would have turned left into Campbell and he'd meet them head on as he came round the corner. Shit, jack. Hesitating still, and yet, if he didn't move soon, he would never get back in fifteen minutes. He thought of the Vacuum. Commitment, Urgency, he told himself, and maybe it was just too wet for the nonnos. He started to run.

He made it out to Scholes. Deserted. There were no verandahs here and the rain coming hard, the big drops smashing into the pavement, lumps of glass, and slashing cold through his hair and the thin denim of his jeans. He ran north for the intersection with Campbell, pushing himself and scared of slipping. The water worming down his neck and jacket stiff and creaking with his effort. Round the corner. He paused in the lee of an old warehouse, breathing hard. No sign of the jackers. Nor of the bulls. Towards Richmond nothing moved except the rain, dancing on the roadway in the yellow light and drumming on the roofs of the parked cars.

Alley Two North was across the street and twenty metres to the right of where he stood, a dark cleft of shadow. On the wet side, sure, except that now the burst of rain was easing. Touch of luck. Spit's luck, he thought. The Attitude. Uniqueness.

Across the street to the corner of the alley. Stopped again. To his right along Scholes, the cars hissed over the wet tarmac. Three steps, four, into the darkness, pressing himself against the wall. What was he scared of? Nobody. Nobody scared Spit. Except Tobin, maybe. Somewhere. Tobin had to come from somewhere.

Further down the alley was a clump of garbage cans. He could just see the curves of them, the grey shape in the streetlights. He peered beyond them at the dark. Nothing moved. His right hand feeling for the package in his jacket pocket. The corners of the little cube pressed sharp through his gloves. Adventure? Shit, jack, wristic bloody wonder. Shivering. And a sound then, suddenly. Or movement. He felt it somewhere – a shift of cold or light or weight, he couldn't tell. He stood, staring, willing his eyes to see.

"Tobin?"

Then a real noise, scuffle, grunt, a let out hiss of breath, a clang and clatter from the tumbling garbage cans. The sound of footsteps moving quickly, running. Away.

"Tobin?" he called again and took a step and then a couple more. His right foot hit a soft thing, flop, which slithered quickly over his boot and then clamped his ankle in a heavy grip. Fuck it! Like a gutrip. Hand, it was a hand, he could see it, and beyond a dark shape, then a face and it was looking up at him. A dud with wide eyes and an open, gaping mouth. A groan.

"Are you Tobin?" Spit asked.

Rattle, like garbled words, from the dud's mouth. Spit bent down to hear.

"Did Blyss send you?" the dud said. No, Spit thought, not right. It doesn't go that way. The dud groaned and twisted, let go of Spit's ankle. Suddenly, he gave a spasm, clutching his chest, a cough and out through his lips came a big spurt of black, something black like paint pouring down his chin. Oh, heavy shit, jack. Spit knew what it was.

And ran.

Back across Campbell and into Scholes, left along the pavement, rain pouring now again, boots in the puddles as he crossed out into the roadway, didn't care, with the cars blasting at him. Horns blaring, wheels scything through the sheets of water. Lights of Jackson blinking up ahead. And right again, the panic pumping in his legs. Oh, shit! Oh, fuck! Oh, help me, holy screaming help me!

The shuttle entrance there on Nelson Street. He was down the steps into the grey light, the tiled echoes, corridor with battered posters on the wall for Dandybars and Jug Wine and *Bland* magazine, the splatters of graffiti. 'Welf and Proud'. And 'Jessers suck'. And 'Strike NOW' shit. Panting, he was panting. Stopped and stood there.

Holy, holy screamer, just like that. The dud's mouth spewing blood. Was dead, wasn't he? He died just then. Spit knew it, he could tell. He watched the fucker die. Or maybe he was still alive back there, in pain and groaning in the alley, needing help. But not with all that blood, though. No. Like a flood of it, a gutsful. Like he was throwing up his life. Like spewing everything. Spit closed his eyes and tried to squeeze the image out. And shit, he should go back, maybe, help the poor gee. No. That was just too crazy. Even if he wanted to, even if he had the guts to look that alley in the face, it made no sense. The bulls'd fit him up for good. He knew that, knew that, knew.

There was a queue at the ticket box. He stood there shivering, thinking, looking for the Vacuum, the strength of it; he needed it, jack, oh how, but it wouldn't come, not even empty words. Two back from the window, he remembered he had no money. Had to use his welfid card, even though they could trace him with it. Fumbling in his inside pocket with his gloved fingers. Nothing. Took off the glove and tried again. Still nothing. Card had gone. It couldn't be. He stood there, unbelieving, helpless, staring, until he remembered then the long, thin, bony fingers patting at him, twitching his lapels.

The dud behind him nudged him in the back. Slowly, he turned away from the ticket box, wandered over towards the vending machines. His boots ascuff through the wash of plastic bottles, boxes, greasy paper bags. A notice on the wall in big red letters: KEEP YOUR SUBWAY CLEAN By Order, District Pride Committee, Petone Borough Council. Some cool calamity had put a fist through it. Walk, he thought. I'll have to walk it home. Three k and he was wet enough already, jeans tight sticking to his legs, his jacket heavy with its sodden shoulder pads. And then, tomorrow, get another card and face the forms, the questions, shit, the heavy stuff. And find a story, jack, so good they'd drop that shit about demerit points. And the black blood gouting in an endless replay in his mind.

Then he remembered, the package. He took it out, a little thing in neatly folded paper, present like the dud said. Tissue paper wrapping gone all slimy with the wet and it slipped off easy, skin like a rotten fruit. A little box of pale blue cardboard with a snugly fitting lid. A jewel maybe. Fuck, he thought. That shithole owes me something. Carefully, the lid. He wriggled it and it came loose, gently lifted off.

A piece of red satin with a thing on it, a round thing, white and glistening with little red veins and a dot, a circle, coloured disc. He touched it, slimy, and it turned in his fingers, slipping on the satin, and he suddenly saw it. There it was, looking up at him.

2

PNPC Profits Up

Port Nicholson Police Company has announced an interim profit of $3.6 million for the six months up to 31st July, slightly up on the result predicted three months ago. General Manager Balder Swensen put the improved position down to an increase in 'operational productivity'. The introduction last year of PNPC's new Support and Surveillance System has proved even more effective than anticipated. Arrest rates are up 15% and convictions 5%. PNPC now tops its two rivals Hutt Law Enforcement and Tawa Police and Penal in the metropolitan statistics. Swensen's emphasis on technology in his three years at the helm seems to have paid off handsomely and the stage looks set for some aggressive bidding in the upcoming local body contract round.

Kim Tokia, business correspondent
Full Financials

Lavendar Tempest woke with the Slumberouser, reached out and turned it off, lay staring into the dark. Around her the world was silent, humless even, as if the whole building and the city beyond it were empty. And the dream? There was a dream but it had gone away, night like a blank wall behind her. Best to keep your back to it, she thought. Just face the morning, yet another empty morning; nothing to start with, everything to gain.

Get going, then!

She rolled back the covers, swung her feet to the floor. Stood up, breathed in deeply in the dark. Monday. Another

Monday. Another week. And it was not so bad. A little more progress every day. And there could be joy in that, surely, whatever the dream was.

Her hand reached out and touched the wall. Turn the light on? No. She could do it in the dark, the whole thing. Beginning in the dark. Like she wouldn't have to be visible till she was ready. Not fit to be seen, not yet. Her robe on the hook behind the door. She dragged it on over her pyjamas, feet into the slippers. Knew exactly where she'd left them too. A nice thing, habits so precise. Because you had to be careful, especially in the mornings, when just the teeniest, tiniest step in the wrong direction could plunge you back into all that darkness.

"No," she said out loud, and opened the door, crossed her little living room and through into the kitchen. Light on now and blinking in the brightness. She flicked the tea switch on the Morning Maker and stood staring at her shadow image reflected in the window. Smooth round of her head and in its face the morning lights of the city coming on. Dawn a greyish smudge behind the black towered silhouettes. Her city. Ten years she'd been here and every day she was a little more sure of herself.

She turned to the wall vid, flicked it into her regular selection, morning news; headline shots on politics and business, followed by fashion and living, new ideas for life and so on.

The report on the Combined Council deficit was creating the usual hoo-hah and the ZIGs were making satisfactory mileage out of it. There were murders up in Petone, more non-people getting killed on the street. The woman from the Hutt Police Company was talking about a ring war. Edmond Eliades and Hamish Duncannen had made a joint statement on tax rationalisation.

She remembered then that she had a dinner date tonight with a young man who said he worked on Eliades corporate staff; a secretary, he claimed. Curtis Caid, his name was, and she had only known him for a few days. He was serious looking and he seemed smart, and ambitious. She didn't usually go out on dinner dates on such short acquaintance but he had intrigued her and, when they had compared their schedules, tonight was the only night in three weeks that they both had free. It would certainly be useful to get a little closer to Eliades.

The Morning Maker gave a soft hiss, let the tea flow (Reliably Prepared to your Exact Specifications. Isn't that nice?) into the cup. She took a sip of it and smiled, thought of her day, as busy as it ought to be. A session at the gym, a work review with her assistant, Simon, a string of other meetings with clients, including one with that gorgeous hunk Mark Bullington, and, in amongst it all somewhere, a special treat. Would she have time for one?

Today would be a good day. Of course, it would be.

Then she noticed Wilfred, sitting there on the bench in his pot; she'd forgotten him entirely.

"Poor you," she said. "You nearly didn't get any breakfast."

She took the jar and the tweezers down from the windowsill, unscrewed the lid, lifted out one of the little nuts of food. It really did look like a little black insect, tiny legs curled up beneath it. Carefully, she lowered it towards a pair of Wilfred's upstretched feeder leaves, dropped it in. The leaves closed smoothly, like a pair of hands, the finger spikes locking together as if pleading, praying. Always a little thrill just to watch them do that. More of a thrill perhaps if the food were alive.

"That's the problem with a new apartment," she said. "There aren't any real insects for you. But you don't mind, do you?" She fed another pair of leaves, imagined what it would be like to be embraced by such a thing, to have it closing round you, locking you in. Which was why it was called a Venus plant, of course. And maybe love was like that, a warm cosiness that wrapped you around and then digested you with its juices. She remembered the words of a song from somewhere.

> A love that is warm and soft and real
> That locks you in its arms of steel

She shuddered. Horrible thought. But a salutary warning, even so. Love was not an option she should ever consider.

The wall vid was running through its lifestyle selection.

"See," she said to Wilfred. "You made me miss the fashions."

But she wasn't annoyed, not really. She was content, in fact, comfortable, sipping the last of her tea and watching the ads for new psychologies roll by and thinking how interesting it would be if you could have pet plants that talked, and how perhaps she should mention it to one of her clients who was in the entertainment technology business and see if they couldn't add it to their bio-computing research program.

And what would Wilfred say, if he could talk?

– Good morning, Lavendar. How nice to see you. You're looking especially pleased with yourself this morning. Let's get to know each other a little better. Why don't you tell me about yourself?

"Nothing to tell," she said aloud.

But then, of course, there was. These days there was. A whole past. Two pasts at the moment. Except that although she still had seven days to choose between them, she knew already, in her heart of hearts, that she didn't want the Hawkes Bay Haven. It had been an interesting little fancy to imagine herself coming from a rural setting but not one that could be made personally viable. She was much more at home with a modified Lambton in which her mother was an eye surgeon and her father a well-known journalist. They were both travelling overseas at the moment but she had been hearing from them regularly since signing up with the Real Biographies programme.

"Perhaps I'll have another message today," she said. "And some pictures of Venice. Wouldn't that be nice?"

And she still had a lot of work to do on her sister, of course. Maybe that would be today's treat, if she could fit it in.

She rinsed her cup under the tap and left it in the sink. Daylight through the window now. The sun bright in the sky over towards Petone but angling in under the cloud cover, which meant it wouldn't last long.

In the bathroom, she dropped her dressing gown to the floor, stepped out of her slippers, took off her pyjamas. With the door and the shower closed she was surrounded by mirrors. Six of them floor to ceiling that reflected her, reflected her reflections. It was a silly idea this bathroom, of course, but she liked it. Liked to focus on this moment of herself at the start of the day. The lines of figures, radiating outwards; the angles of them, arrowing into their different distances. Like a star, like her being, with each line a set of possibilities, a future starting here at this moment, and all coordinated, synchronised with her slightest movement now.

She looked over her body, the morning's critical survey. One hundred and seventy centimetres, sixty-two kilograms. Breast ninety-one, waist sixty-three, hips ninety. Skin pale, white, a milky white. It was this year's complexion almost exactly and she was pleased about that. Skin toning was expensive. Well, easy enough to get a rough approximation, of course, but if you wanted to be comfortable with the precise hint of blue or yellow, it could cost you a bundle and a deal of pain to go with it. Shoulders. Her shoulders were good, square, assertive, strong. She never wanted to compromise on the shoulders. Always had a pride in herself and always knew what she wanted, that was what the shoulders said. A bit bony maybe but...

In profile. All the thousands of Lavendars turned their heads to look at the thousands of Lavendars around them. A good straight carriage (Wanderman's Spinal Technique for Total Well-being, thank you, sir), a tummy nicely flat and breasts with a lift. She had good breasts (well, they had cost enough) and buns too. Yes. Were the legs too skinny? Just a touch more flesh at the back of the thigh there? No, no. It was all right. She gave a little curtsy to herself like a dancer and the corps de ballet curtsied back. (Well, we all approve, don't we? And we all applaud.)

Was it vanity? No, she didn't think so. For vanity was vanus, Latin for empty, and she couldn't think of herself as empty. She was full of purpose and ambition. And if she chose to manage herself in a way which best fulfilled her goals, then that was good, wasn't it? Because the theory said (and who was she to contradict it?) that the body was your meeting with the world, your interface. And what people saw they projected onto you, so your appearance always, in their eyes, was a part of each of them; and so you managed your appearance in a way that called out of them the responses they should give you. And it worked, didn't it?

Well, sometimes. And she only had to think of what she looked like then, ten years ago. Except she wasn't going to think about that.

She stepped into the shower and turned it on. Warm immediately with its winter setting. Shampoo for the short spiky hair over her head and then soaping her arms and body, legs. Thinking through her appointments, her day, and what she was going to wear. Serious, she thought, the navy blue. And the hair? Why not be a little daring with that? A tawny blonde, perhaps? Well, yes, she thought so.

◊

The Ratman asleep at the workbench, head down across the arms among the flickering screens, the headsets, mikes, printers, inputs, old-fashioned keyboards. Scattering of papers, cardboard, food containers, blo-glo cups and cast-off lids. Working all night and before that working, hooked into the fix, the headset clamped over the skull, the channels live with sound and image, fingers fluttering on pads and voice that chants the answers, never ceasing, busy, busy, have to, have to, more, more, more. Until, at last, it slumps, exhausted.

And dreams.

The Ratman dreams of water.

Long cool stretch of lake a blue, grey, silver smooth beneath a silver sky. The slopes leading down are dark with pine trees. Voices clear and high like bells are calling, children down along the shore among the smooth white stones. It is morning or evening, light with lift or fade and the Ratman watches from its keep, its brain alive, the brain's eyes wide and staring, thoughts behind them scampering still like things on little treadmills, never stopping.

– Hey, Ratman.

Voice in the head, the signal coming in from somewhere.

– You on-line, man?

– Who that? Ratman asks.

Stirring now, its eyes opening. Shit, shit, shit.

– Foxy, man.

Foxy gives a jazz pattern through the video.

– Hi, Foxy.

– What you got on that new bio-chip? The SVD9270?

– Specs not out yet.

– Bubby says he got it.

– Bubby? Bullshit.

– Says so.

– Conning you, man. Anyway, Ratman don't do hardware. You know that.

– I thought, maybe. Just in case.

– Talk to Bubby.

– Bubby's off-line.

– Ratman off-line too.

– See you, Ratman.

Ratman didn't go, though. Waited. Listening to the dark, watching the dark. Grey-blue flicker deep down in the video.

– Give the Ratman something hard to do. Need something to do.

But nothing. No one there. So it sat up then. Flipped the visor, looked around. The screens all going, hum from the drives. Rustle in the food-wrappings. Something alive in there. And dumb old Foxy. Never got it right, how Ratman only did the logic: models, math, and modules, procedures, protocols, and polydifferential parallels. Fingers in the beard and twisting, stuffed a handful of it in the mouth and chewed, a rough tough, crunchy. Tasted of ketchup, old ketchup. Popped a couple of pills then, downed them with cold coffee.

– Hello there, boy.

Knew this one, though. Charlie Cato, Bossman. Back again when he was wanted. Ratman flipped the visor down and saw Charlie's logo, red lightning from a blue-green cloud.

– Hi, Charlie.

– Got two for you.

– Goody, goody. Send them down, Charlie.

– Can't do the first one on-line. It's a local.

– Who?

– Southern Information Systems. Intracity Network.

– What they want?

– They got a hacker.

– Don't want hackers, Charlie. Don't want that shit. Give me something hard.

– This is hard, boy. You better believe it. Head of Ops there, Mary Yeadon. She'll call.

– Will, will, will.

– The second one's an integration seam. New Bank of Beijing. Spec and a visual. You want them?

– Okey-dokey.

Came in a bundle. Mind focused on it, felt the size, complexity. Layers of information, intuition folding round it. Big, but seeable, knowable. Deep you had to go in a thing like this. A thing, a thing. Saw the logic of it and the spec. Saw too that it didn't quite fit. It was a forceps knot. Every way you looked it was a forceps knot. Which was dumb, which was crazy. Why they do it like that? Any silly, dumb, dumb see it wouldn't, couldn't, shouldn't. So?

Just rest it for a bit.

Sat up. Stood up. Stood there, breathing slow, to practice breathing slow, and took a walk to the door and back. Sticky something on the carpet, spilled there. Yes, the coffee. Knocked it when? Was when?

And something local, Charlie said. A hacker. Didn't like a hacker. Real world, world outside. Ratman didn't like the world outside and never went there now. Well, not if it could help it. Last time when? Twelve meals. Six sleeps. Something, didn't know precisely. Took the lift to fifty, walked the tubestreet to Maui Plaza. Weirdy, weirdy night-lit sky was all around and glowing through the rain-slashed tunnel. Got the shakies, then, though, vertigo and thinking how an earthquake, big one, all come tumbling down. Ratman scuttled back to the room before the vomit came. It was dizzy, in a panic.

There in a blank screen, movement of the reflection, little figure, naked Ratman, dark in the curved glass, drifting left to right. Stepped towards it and it loomed. Click, turned on, the monster gone now. Didn't like reflections. Made you look and see. Better instead to have the screens working, stuff happening. Anything happening.

Integration seam. The forceps knot. Was easy. Forceps knot was all crap, needed a double loop in there and any sucky knew it wouldn't work otherwise. Let's do the figuring. Ratman do the work. And charge old Charlie a million dollars worth. Look at the spec. A four-line change, see? And when that was done there was just a little bit of logic in the three exception routines. All right, my matey. Aren't you the genius, then?

◊

The sound of gunfire, mushy, distant. Spit groaned and turned over. Burst of music, bugle call, the cavalry, the cavalry! He opened his eyes and stared at the window, grey with daylight. Shots again and a commentary, the music wrenching hearts now. He hated that pissdick stuff on the morning news, so persistent, jolly, cheerful. PJC.

He had to get up, anyway. If he lay in bed for another day like he was tempted, head under the blankets, pretending he was slimed, the FAM would call the healthers for sure. And then they'd find out he didn't have a pissing card. And the thought of the card reminded him. A tall, thin dud whose name was Blyss with bony fingers, long like spiders' legs, his knobby knuckles. Smiling. And the black blood spewing out of the dud's mouth. More than a day ago now, a day and two nights, and yet he still saw it, heard it even, that soft, hot gush. And the eye looking up at him.

An explosion.

He sat up.

The noise was from the next room, seeping through the cardboard wall. The Farter sitting, fat, in his fat chair with the sagging springs. His worried eyes. His belly swelling in his threadbare T-shirt. And Spit with a hollow feeling of despair. He couldn't face the geries, not today. Their helplessness, their welfarse worrying, their soghead plans on how to spend their time.

– Shall we watch the TV, Maudie?

– After we've done the learning options, dear. Then, later on, we can go downstairs and have a beer.

– Two beers. We can afford two beers, can't we?

Dead, jack, dead and SKB. They were dead from the neck up. No pissing wonder the Hutt was full of geribashers. Where was the energy? The hunger? Shit, you had to do something, get out of here. C for commitment and U for urgency.

He swung his legs over the edge of the bed, winced as his bare feet touched the cold concrete. The central heating still not fixed. He scrabbled for his shoes.

"Maudie!" The Farter's voice, worried. Something had got to him. The news announcer's drone without the music, now. Important stuff, it must be. End of the pissing world with luck.

"Maudie!" The edge of panic.

Spit put on his jeans, a tricky manoeuvre which involved taking each foot out of its shoe, sliding it down the thin black tube of denim, still damp from the rain of then, and slipping it back into the shoe without his toes touching the floor. He should wear something else, a change of touch, new role but what the fuck. He wasn't going to do that full droppo number anyway. Just the jeans along with socks and sneakers and an old cotton skivvy with his bomber jacket. Needed to look the scruff. Needed to scam a breakfast out of somebody. So it was a new touch, then, in a way. He felt better about that.

Outside in the corridor. The lift was working, miracle. He stood inside it, hands in his jacket shivering. So bloody cold; or it was just him maybe, squirming at the touch of Blyss's fingers. But he didn't care. This dud can hack it. The lift shook and rattled like it was twisted out of shape and didn't fit in the shaft any more. The metal walls covered in wild sprays of paint and layers of letters peeling thick. A white paper notice stuck on at an angle: NO GRAFFITI by Order of the Naenae Welfare Housing Committee. Some freak had tagged it with a single word: Fuk. Well, what did you expect?

Had to get down the campus first, of course. Jank would be there and maybe she could help him talk a good story through and get it straight before he went and flopped in the offices and confessed that he had dropped his card. Those welfare psychobutchers had special training to tell when you were lying and they'd want to know the whole pissing thing. Whatever he told them, he had to believe it himself. It was the only way. Everybody knew that.

There were huddles of nonnos along the street. In twos and threes and fours, around the corners and tucked into doorways. Silent, watching, always watching. Eyes to right and left. Spit would have walked on by on a normal morning. They were always there, invisible. Today, though, he was worried about eyes and the slam-brained shadows of the nonno world where the real gizzoes were. He had been there now. He had seen it. And not just the fringe stuff like Gag the Cutman who hung around the school canteen doing odd jobs and selling the kids his special sniff or fudge or screamers if you were clobbed enough to want them. Spit had seen Tobin in the alley. He had seen the blood and the eye in the little box had looked at him. That was ringland biz. It had to be. He felt a flick of fear in his belly. And something else, too. A kind of pride. A mark of favour. An ASP was made by the secrets he never told.

3

Fee's New Beau?

'Who's the hunk?' This was the question on everyone's lips last night as City Supergirl Fiona Duncannen stepped out into the slick time at Sleepers night club with an unknown beefy on her arm. Dressed in a skin-hugging suit of gold synxette, the Port Nick Princess danced the night away with her blond big-boy while the Rich and Beautiful wondered who he was and where he'd sprung from. Well, babes, wonder no more! *Pump Trend* is here to tell you that those gorgeous pecs in the Dead Rep T shirt belong to none other than aspiring holographer Saigo Bruce whose opening next week at The Trout Gallery is certain now to attract a tad more attention than he might otherwise have hoped for. Sexy Saigo spent the whole night gazing into the eyes of the Ever-Gorgeous Fee and who can blame him? But is this true love, friends? Or is our sculptor in light no more than a cheap chiseller out for Daddy's billions?

Pump Trend

Isis Image Management, Suite 703, 45th floor, Colosseum North East Tower. A small place. Small? It was tiny but Lavendar didn't mind that, not really. Just to have her own company, one that was successful and growing, was enough satisfaction, for the time being at least. And in practical terms, it didn't matter what size the premises were, as long as they had a decent address. Eighty percent of the business was done over the videophone these days and the rest was lunches and meetings which could just as easily be conducted off site in a quiet restaurant or a room hired from the Business Centre.

She and Simon needed very little space, just an office each, a meeting cubicle and the little reception area for deliveries and the occasional visitor.

She sat down at her desk and turned on the two- by three-metre vid on the wall opposite. It would have been nice to have an actual view out of a real window but the vid was almost as good. Today it showed the harbour and the Eastbourne shore in the far distance, a natural, real-time scene of mist and rain and low scudding, wind driven sea. She could have chosen something prettier or more scenic, a Manhattan skyline or a view of the Andes, for example, but she was superstitious about anything that took her beyond her present circumstances.

Whatever her prospect was, it had to be relevant. It had to be grounded in her real life. You are here, this view said. This is where you operate, what you work with. And, in any case, there was absolutely nothing wrong with a view out over Aotea Quay, was there? It was just as impressive as one of the great cityscapes of the Northern Hemisphere, more so these days. No need to pretend. No need to hide. No need to make excuses.

She called Simon and brought up his image in the lower right of the vid. "Good morning," she said. "You're up and about early."

"You know me. Always striving for the common good. How was the gym?" He gave his impish grin and tossed his long black hair out of his eyes. He was cultivating an ascetic look these days, or was it aesthetic? Both probably. The Romantic Poet studying Buddhism.

"As it should be," she answered. "What's happening here?"

"Everything's under control. Gordan Sapich called. I filed him for you. And Mark Bullington cancelled. Says will Wednesday at nine do? Get back to his secretary if not."

Annoying. Very. Famous clients always assumed you were at their beck and call. So patronising.

"I've ordered you coffee," Simon said. A concerned look, seeing her irritation. It made her feel better at once.

"Thank you. Can we run our review this afternoon? Four-thirty or so."

"No problem."

When he had gone she called up Gordan's message. His face tanned, blond hair cropped short, eyes a pale blue. Smiling. A handsome man, Gordan, she had always thought so.

"Lavendar," he said. "Just a quick word to thank you for all the effort you've put into the Gala promotion. Everything looks set for a really great evening tomorrow. I'll see you there."

Which was nice. Really nice to be appreciated by someone in Gordan's position, even if he was also an old friend. It was so curious how life worked, how you could meet someone at university and like them for their own sake, and then, suddenly, they're up and coming in the world, the secretary of the newest and most vigorous political party, and you're getting little benefits from that connection which you really never expected. Not that you didn't deserve them though. No, not at all.

There was a flicker in the lower right corner of her vid and a window opened showing the outer office, the coffee boy standing there in his uniform, yellow with maroon piping, a little military-style cap like an upturned boat perched on his head. She stood up, moved around her desk towards the door and opened it with perfect timing as the boy raised his hand to knock.

"Hello," she said.

"Double long Kenyan, ma'am?"

"Exactly right." He was a cute kid with ginger hair and a rosy pink complexion. She took the white blo-glo cup from his hand and smiled at him.

"Is that charge?" he asked, awkward.

"Of course. Thank you so much."

And suddenly, he blushed to the roots of his spiky hair. Whatever is he thinking of? she thought as she closed the door.

◊

Jank was in the basement where the lockers used to be. Leaning against the wall in her droppo gear, doing nothing. Droppoes spent a lot of time leaning against walls doing nothing. It was a kind of art with them.

"Hey, buzz," Jank said. "Where you bin?"

"Hi, buzz." Slipping into the lingo.

"Lost you Satday. Figged you musta had your own idea."

"Yer." And Spit realised suddenly there was no way he could tell Jank about it. Not yet, anyway. Not ever, maybe. "Got any clink?" he asked.

"You kiddin? This is Monday, buzzer."

"Got any creds, then. I'm busted, broke. I need some breakfast."

"Get you a shit and water." It was the campus droppoes' term for a cup of canteen coffee.

"Thanks, buzz."

The same old boring morning, jack. The canteen with its scattered tables and plastic chairs, the grubby green walls dotted with posters, not allowed but nobody gave a shit that much, the smell of yesterday's stale slop gutsful, foul like boiled cabbage and rotten mutton. They got two coffees at the servery. Jank paid with her welfid card. The fat woman behind the till kept staring at Spit as if she knew something; so he stared her back, the greasy slink with her sour, mouthdown bulldog expression, until she turned away and pretended she was interested in Gag the Cutman, who was cleaning up out back, flicking a dirty looking rag over the stainless steel surfaces.

Jank wanted to join a bunch of droppoes at a table over by the window, but Spit thought shit on that and slid her to a spot where they could sit by themselves. The place was empty apart from the droppoes and a few lonelys here and there. The academic wheels were grinding away upstairs and all the gungs would be up in the L-bays soaking up the fresh, new daily dollops of crap that were being dished out.

"So, buzz." Jank was watching him, waiting. She'd picked something was going on.

"I dropped my card," Spit said.

"Hey, buzzer!" Her eyes widened in surprise and shock. "How you do that?"

"I just dropped it. I was in a bar, Saturday. You know. I think some wrister fingered it."

"Who? Who, buzz?"

"Some tall thin dud in a suit. Blond." No more, Spit told himself. Jank couldn't help. She didn't need to know.

"A suit, buzz? Why he do that?"

"I don't know, jack. What am I going to do about it, that's the point? I can't tell 'em where I was, can I?"

"Wow!" Jank shook her head in amazement and Spit felt depressed. It was useless talking to droppoes. They were just too pissing amiable to think straight. Terminally inoffensive. No wonder they got slammed on.

"Wow!" Jank said again and stared helplessly over to her sibs by the window. Well, maybe they should come over. Maybe they could tumble one decent idea between them. There was a scraping of chairs as if the droppoes had got the message by telepathy.

Spit didn't look as they gathered round and sat down. There were six of them and they drew in close and put their elbows on the table. He felt crowded all of a sudden and he knew for sure that his thing with Jank was coming to an end. Whatever the hell his next ASP role was, it would be with duds who didn't huddle.

"Hey, buzz," one of the droppoes said.

"Buzzer dropped his card," Jank explained. "A suit slipped it."

A chorus of wows. Amazed looks. Shaking heads.

"What he do, buzz?" Jank demanded.

"Wow, buzzer," someone said.

"Hey, buzz," said another. "A suit, you reck?"

"Yer, jack."

"Thin suit? Blond hair? Name of Blyss?"

Spit felt a strange sense of cold creep over him, like his skin was alive and trying to get away.

36

"Maybe," he said.

"He onto you, buzz. This morning. Yesterday. Sometime." Spit couldn't speak.

"How, buzz? What he say?" Jank asked.

"He was asking for Arlen. Arlen the Spit, the droppo, buzz. Something like that. It was this morning. Down by the Kings Parlour. That the one?"

"Maybe."

"Wow!"

"Hey, buzz!"

"Hey, buzzeroo!"

The round eyes, the shaking heads, the soft, gentle voices. The belch of blood from the dud's mouth, the blond man's spider fingers tickling on his skin. And a sick cold panic in his guts.

"I gotta go, jack," he said, standing up, flinging his chair back.

"See ya, buzzer."

"Kings Parlour, buzzboy. That the one."

Spit went for the door, quickly, almost running, slammed it back and through into the corridor beyond. To his left the brown linoleum stretched down a long slot of paint-tagged concrete to the basement doors with their reinforced glass panels, distant squares of light. Attitude, he told himself. Was attitude that counted. Think like a slick, like a scammer with the way on. He set off brisk towards the light. The viper strikes. To hell with panic, jack.

"Hey, boy!" A boom of voice behind him. He stopped, turned. A tall thin figure in a flapping coat was hobbling after him. For a moment he thought... But then he saw who it was.

"Don't you rush off, boy." Gag the Cutman, panting and grinning, his trousers too big for him and sloshing round his skinny legs, his grey dust-coat filthy stained with old washed grease marks and chemicals. Spit waited as the shambling rush caught up with him and wondered what the fuck. Because he never dealt with the Cutman, never in the normal way, except a nick of fudge maybe but any dud did that.

Gag loomed over him, a hollow-eyed and grinning, blotchy face. His teeth were rotten stumps. "I got a message for you, boy."

"From Blyss?"

"Don't know. Not sayin. But if you want to talk to your man, you be at the Colosseum tonight, seven-thirty. North End, level 18. A place called Candy's."

"The Colosseum? That's in Nicholson. Downtown. I can't go there. I got no card, no money, nothing."

"Sssh!" Gag said, a finger to his lips, a long finger with a grimy nail. The other hand, like a drooping bird's beak, was reaching out, holding something. Spit offered his palm. A little clink and a flash of light, the weight of the coins still warm from Gag's grip. Four of them, a brassy yellow, twenty dollar bits.

"Be there, boy. North End, level 18," Gag said, turning away, and added, over his shoulder. "And that's advice."

◊

Buzz from the videophone, a call coming in. Popped a pill and pressed the vision button. Woman, blonde with narrow jaw and red lips, blue eyes. Skin pale, nose thin, little flare of the nostrils. Wow, a sexy piece, a lucky Ratman got to look at you and got to talk to, too. Could it talk to? Wasn't sure. It was scared a bit.

"Mary Yeadon," she said.

"Yes, y-y-yes." Waited. For her to say but she didn't. Suddenly, the screen went blank.

"Pictures both ways," she said. "Or we don't talk."

Ratman pressed the video release so she could see. Who cared, if she didn't? Beard and hair, black hair. There was lots of hair. And naked, but she wouldn't pick that from just the chest and shoulders.

"Okay." Her image came back. Red mouth, didn't smile. Looking at the Ratman and not caring, seeing what it looked like. Didn't bother her a bit. "You're Richard Pope?"

"Y-yes."

"You know who I am?"

"Y-y-yes. Mary Yeadon, Intracity N-n-n-networks. Hacker."

"Hackers. How do you want it? A verbal briefing or the data."

"T-t-talk," Ratman said. From a sexy piece, why not? "And d-data later."

"We've got a big network here. Big and old. Lots of technology, layers of it. Most of it still in use somehow, somewhere. We've got copper and microlinks and fibre optics. There's data moving in streams and packets and Feynmann tunnels. There's over five hundred thousand nodes and upwards of three million users. It's all just grown. And without any real ownership. None of the customers want centralised control of anything. Southern runs it but everybody has a piece of it, all going their own ways and strutting their stuff. And because the latest design systems have computer enhanced complexity control they can get away with it. Well, almost."

"S-sure. Seen it before."

"But not this bad, I'll bet. Our current problem is that we've got hackers, at least one, playing games and doing a little fraud and we can't track them down."

"G-g-games?"

"Playing with AV transmissions and e-mail. Doing funny little things to TV programmes and on-line movies. Concocting messages which seem to be getting into restricted domains."

"And the CBF?" F was for fraud and also for funny. Fin, fan, funny.

"Example. Somebody ordered a pile of hardware from Startech Corporation, paid for it from an account owned by the Church of the New Enlightenment and got it delivered to an address in Hutt City that we can't trace. Another, somebody cleaned out a bank account belonging to a Tawa businessman, Fatsuo Molle. We can't find out where the money went. Which is a problem because Mr Molle is the kind of person who takes losing money especially hard."

"T-t-tricky." And sticky and picky and tough, tough bicky.
"I could go on," Yeadon said.
"N-n-no. Give the data. What you got?"

Cockroach, fat one, ran across her face. It was quick. But smack! Got it. Lay there in the keyboard, legs up, wriggling. Worm of guts on the screen beside Yeadon's nose. A little goldy wiggly with the light shining through. A gleaming little wiggle. Wiped it off with the side of the wrist.

"Interesting place you've got there," she said.
"J-j-j-just me."
"I want a report tonight." Image fade.
"And yes, yes, yes. And good, good, good."

The Ratman never sleeps.

4

Killer Sound Comes On Strong

A new wave of retch music is taking the sewer clubs by storm.

Smooth and Blues is dead, jack! Long Live Split Head Rock!

Taking advantage of the new low end megamp power doublers and wrap video folders, today's City bands are dumping the sly sentiment of recent months and roaring through the glens with a fresh wind of change. Big Noise is in and the windows are rattling along Wakefield Street.

The new wave has the City Health killjoys scrabbling for their close orders already. Like standing next to a jet engine, one crud told me. Is that right, sister? Bet you suck sweeties to the Bland Brothers, don't you?

The rats, on the other, hand are lapping it up. 'It's a riot', one fan told me. 'It makes my nose bleed.' Death by Sound lead mixer Paula Flesch says the new groups are just high on power. 'Fuck that smooth shit. We're into guts, jack.'

All over the footpath, honey child!

Mack Flack, special correspondent
City Sense

Madeleine Drummond, personality consultant from Real Biographies, smiled at her from the wall vid. "Lavendar, I didn't expect to see you again so soon."

"Someone cancelled on me and I thought, well, why not indulge myself for once?"

"That's the ticket."

A curious, old world expression, Lavendar thought, but then Madeleine was a curious, old world sort of person. A white blouse, frilly collar high at the neck, hair pulled back tight in a bun. Like a school teacher from one of those TV series about the pioneers. But a sweet face, even if the nose was a little pointy.

"I have your file right here," Madeleine said. "You've been doing so well with it. But then, of course, you would appreciate the delicacy required, given your own work."

Lavendar smiled at the compliment. "Oh, what I do is much more functional. Straightforward really."

She settled herself back in her chair and folded her hands in her lap, as another window opened beside Madeleine's face. There was a tiny flicker in it and then the Lambton logo bloomed; a skyscraper with a red rose across it.

"Now, where were we?" Madeleine asked. "Cynthia, wasn't it?" Cynthia's picture replaced the logo, full face and profile. Dark hair, high cheek-bones, narrow jaw.

"We really hadn't got much beyond this, had we?" Madeleine said. "How does it look today?"

"A bit haggard perhaps."

"Yes, perhaps. But then she is, what? Three years older than you?"

"Four. She used to push me around in my stroller when I was a toddler."

"We could maybe have a photo of that, do you think?"

"Or even video."

"A chubby little girl and her baby sister. Where? At the beach."

"Along the Parade."

"Of course. I'll rough something up."

"And I think, probably, she used to feed me my lunch. Out on the deck of the apartment. She was really quite devoted to me."

"You never fought."

"Oh, we did, of course. Many times. But there was never

any jealousy in it. It was always just a clash of wills. We are both very strong personalities, you see. We both go for what we want."

"But never any jealousy."

"No." Lavendar thought about the paradox. But she knew how it was, how her sister had been during all the time of their growing up. "Cynthia's perhaps not quite as determined as I am. She would generally concede, I suppose."

"More considerate?"

"Less headstrong. Wiser. I guess she used to let me have my way when we were young but not through weakness, no. More a kind of acceptance of things. Cynthia has always been able to see into the heart of life and to appreciate that personal ambition does not necessarily guarantee happiness."

"She is wise," Madeleine said.

"And more generous than I am, perhaps. More motherly."

"Does she have children?"

Good lord, what a startling thought! What would it be like to be an auntie? Auntie Lavendar? No, she didn't think so.

"I think she'd like to," she said. "But there are difficulties."

"There are really interesting technologies developing around fertility at the moment," Madeleine went on. "IUC, for example."

"IUC?"

"Inter Uterine Cloning. Perhaps Cynthia might be interested in that."

"No, I'm not sure that's Cynthia's thing. More conservative. More interested in the natural way."

"Earth Mother?"

"A little."

"She'd better carry more weight then."

"And she probably lives in the country now. She enjoys animals and flowers."

"Horses?"

"Oh, yes."

"A little of the Hawkes Bay Haven, then?"

"Yes, of course." And Lavendar realised suddenly why she had chosen to explore that other possibility. "Doesn't it all work out neatly?"

"I generally find it so," Madeleine said.

◊

Tippy, tip, tip sang the little white chip. And the data on the screen went urgle-gurgle. Mad transactions dancing their little dances and the Ratman had to get the head around it, had to feel the shape of it. An all so sloppy problem definition, all that data all in a mess all over. Weird transactions, true. Wonky little spats of stuff that zapped people's TV programmes when they were watching them, turned the apples into golf-balls, maybe, made the mice into monsters. Wormy little worryings that nicked their way into bank accounts and order systems, clicked the zeroes over. See your money? Now it's gone, ha, ha. Ratman saw them all go in and do their stuff, a pattern in the head and Ratman built a model of it, showed it on the screen and proved it, see, see, see. But trouble was, the bubble was, IT DIDN'T KNOW WHERE THE SUCKERS CAME FROM.

There, there, there, the shouty Ratman not so good. And popped a pill to keep it calm, but nothing to swish it down with. Stuck in the throat and went itchy, scritchy, made it bitchy. And messy, mess, mess. It was mess all over. Mess in the head and mess on the bench. So up and doing, walking up and walking down. And found a big old plastic bag and into it went all the paper, cups and cardboard slops, and scrapy, scrape the sticky yuk beside the green screen. Clean, see? A tidy Ratman, sticky but.

And start again. Dialled up the Good Old Burger Bar.

"Two Fatman Specials, a Double Ripple Apple Tub, a litre coke and a black c-c-coffee." Fatman for the Ratman.

"Where to?" Girlie-wirly in the green cap, surly. Ratman be nice to you and you be nice to Ratman, okay?

"95, BG 6, Crossing T-t-t-tower-er-er-er."

"What was that?"

"95, BG 6, C-c-c-c-c-. Lemme see. 95, BG 6, Crossing Tower, 81 Willis." Gottim!

"Charge to?"

"Blaxcred 1972514."

"Enter your pin please."

Did it.

"Thank you, sir. Have a nice day, sir."

And quick, quick, quick, you better be quick, the Ratman had the hungers on. A wobble, wobble, gobble, gobble, tidy Ratman had to, had to, now, now, now.

The problem. Get the problem. Eat the problem. All that data, glup, glup, glup. And Ratman Clever Head, the cunning so-and-so. The problem was... (And don't go shouty!), the problem was... (And are you listening?) We see what happens to all that stuff, its little doings, all the naughties but we don't see where it comes from, eh? We don't see who puts it in there.

So. So, logically, nobody puts it there. It makes it all up by itself. So? So, Mary Yeadon, red lips, who watches squish of cockroaches and doesn't flinch. So, Cool Eyes. Ratman got the answer for you. Stuff your hacker up your knickers, eh? Because this little sucker is a VIRUS! YA!

◊

Three-thirty. Lavendar Tempest walking back from an appointment with the Port Nicholson Basketball Association, strolling through the tubestreet across Willis to Duncannen Central. The weather was as grey and blustery in reality as it looked on her wall vid, streaks of rain wriggling over the tube's transparent surface like luminous worms. Down below, the black canyon far beneath her feet was clogged with traffic. Strange how life had changed since the tubes had been put in. If you lived downtown, as she did, you walked everywhere and you never actually had to descend to street level at all, just passed from building to building at the thirty-fifth storey or so. She had recently read an article in *Solo* which claimed that there was a new mental condition developing in the city. Bathyphobia, it was called, the fear of the depths. Lavendar thought perhaps it sounded more like an aversion to soap and water, but she was willing to give credence to the idea. Sometimes she wondered about herself, how she would survive down there again, if she had to.

Over in Duncannen, she took a turn round the fashion gallery, not really wanting to buy but needing a small break and just to see if there were any new ideas which might give a sign of trends to come. Liking, too, to watch the ghost of her own image flitting over the glass, slim and elegant in the tailored suit, tall in the black patent leather mid-heel shoes. She enjoyed how this ghost of herself moved so confidently and that you couldn't actually see its face. It was the way she thought of herself sometimes, anonymous and insubstantial but such a striking presence nonetheless, mysterious.

She was standing before Mason and Hardinge's looking at the Spring Collection window when her phone rang. She took it out of her bag and flicked it into voice only.

"Hello, Lavendar Tempest speaking."

"Dougall Myerson. Galen Corporation."

Galen? Good heavens, she had never had work from them before.

"How can I help?" she asked, trying to sound calm. Galen was only the biggest provider of medical services to the city. Hospitals, clinics, research....

"One of our people needs coaching for a media statement. He asked for you."

"Oh, and who is that?"

"Carl Robollo."

She hardly knew him. Well, she'd met him once or twice because his wife was on Gordan Sapich's ZIG Gala Organising Committee. Lavendar must have given him her card some time. The shadow in the window with the phone to its ear stared out at her from the centre of a group of mannequins dressed in cream and gold.

"Are you available?" Myerson asked.

"When exactly?"

"Now."

Could she? She had to. "Yes. I think so. I can be back at my desk in five minutes."

"Call me." He hung up.

She dialled into the office system immediately and checked her appointments for the rest of the afternoon. Only one, apart from her review meeting with Simon. Easy enough to change them both. For Galen Corporation? Yes, of course. She thought of Carl Robollo, a sour-looking man, middle-aged with a toneless voice. Certainly a candidate for media coaching. Surely she could make a difference there?

◊

– Hey, Ramesh, how's it going?

– Ratman. Good to touch with you, my friend.

– Need some thinking, Ramesh.

– Thinking? Am I the right fellow for such a thing?

– You the Virus King, man.

– Ah, virus. Virus, maybe.

– Something here. I got a network, big mother. Half a meg of nodes. K of owners. Every kind of hardware. Ding, dong, bell.

– I know the situation.

– I got AV corruption. I got CBF. I can see the transactions but I don't see where they come from. Come from systems don't exist. Come from places have no record. Could it be a little itty, big bitty virus, maybe?

– Could be.

– Where's it hiding, man?

– Could be a roller.

– Don't know roller.

– A roller moves from machine to machine through the network. When it arrives it takes over some of the resources and locks them off. Then it does its stuff, cleans up after itself and moves on.

– Invisible, man?

– A good one is. Only way to tell is by the effects. Or by performance. If you have a roller in a machine, it generally uses so much CPU and memory the whole thing starts to slow down. Same with the network. A roller moving on is like an elephant on the highway.

– Big?

– They're big, my friend.

– Mine must be a big pig just to do the fancy-dancy stuff it's up to.

– I seen them very big.

– A monster, mine.

– I have some stuff if you can use it.

– Thanky, panky, Ramesh.

Flickety, flick and down came all the Great R's info through the video channel, words and numbers, diagrams. There were schemas and plans and models and specs, a cunning little spec for a little tiny roller, show you how to do it, isn't he clever?

Boy, oh boy, I got you monster. Ratman have you tied up double quick.

GeeeeeeeeeeeeeeeeeeeEEEEEEEEERONIMO!!!

◊

Myerson was head of PR. That big. He explained that Carl needed to make public statements on a medical test that had gone wrong. Someone had been having what was called an Electro-Neural Attitude Scan and the equipment had overloaded. A surge of input had sent the patient into a coma. Sensitive. Yes, she could see that. A potential malpractice suit. A scandal, even.

"Carl's our leading expert on electro-neural interfaces. He invented these tests. Unfortunately, he's not very…well, you've met him."

"Dealing with the public isn't his strength?"

"Exactly. You folk do a good job with Carl and maybe there's more work for you. Follow-up stuff."

"Oh, we'll do a good job," she told him.

Robollo came up on her wall vid looking haggard; bags under his eyes, heavy lines around his mouth. She turned him down to less than life size so that these unpleasant little details weren't so obvious.

"Hello, Carl."

"Lavendar. How do we do this?"

"Just tell me what happened."

"Okay."

She waited for him to continue but he seemed uncertain, confused. An old man, she thought, an unhappy old man. Even fixing the wrinkles might not do much about that. Aging was such a melancholy condition.

"Carl, please," she said. "I do need your own words if we're going to keep a lid on this thing. And you will have to lighten up, just a fraction."

"Lighten up? How do you mean?"

"Relax a little, take it easy."

He gave a big sigh and squared his shoulders, wagged his head to ease the tension in his neck. His eyes, though, still looked scared.

"Look at me, Carl. Please." He did so, and she gave him a smile. It was a deliberate smile, calculated, full of amusement, understanding, sympathy. She knew exactly what effect it had on people, especially middle-aged men.

It worked this time, too. Carl Robollo's eyes softened. For a moment it seemed he might burst into tears. Instead, he coughed, rubbed his nose in embarrassment and grinned at her. He looked years younger in a second.

"That's better. That's more like it. Confidence, now. That's what we need. Imagine I'm interviewing you. Now what happened exactly?"

"Well, we had a problem with one of our..."

"Not a 'problem', I think. A situation, maybe."

"A situation arose with one of our new..."

"New? Are these things experimental?"

"No. We're starting to use them quite a lot."

"Standard practice?"

"You could say so."

"'Standard' is much better."

"A situation arose with one of our standard ENAS tests. There appears to have been a technical malfunction which…"

"Didn't Dougall say something overloaded?"

"Yes."

"Then, please, no malfunctions." Dear me, she thought. This is such hard work sometimes.

"It seems that there was an unfortunate build up in one of the input channels. Frank Biling, the technician, killed the…"

"No staff names, please. Let's say…"

"Our fail safe balance system kicked in, of course…"

Lavendar nodded encouragement.

"…but unfortunately not before the patient, Mr Mountain…"

It was all right in the end, after she'd prompted him and coached him and then edited the results into three different statements for different newsbanks. He came across as sincere, open, concerned. Even the last little vestiges of his tension were an advantage, giving the impression that he was just an honest bloke doing his job and that this unusual situation was something an honest bloke just had to cope with.

Once she'd finished with Robollo she dialled into the hospital ward to see if there was an image she could use, but the sight of the victim, Derek Mountain, lying there hooked up to all that equipment was just too heart-rending. All she got was a little clip from one of the team of doctors saying that the patient was resting and under observation.

At six-fifteen she e-mailed the package to Myerson, turned off the media management system and leaned back in her chair. The view through her wall vid was still blustery and wet. Satisfying, really, in its way. An image of struggle which was kept at bay, as if you were standing up to the forces of nature. And prevailing.

And she had prevailed, hadn't she? Well, she had certainly

made the very best of her opportunity. Galen must surely be pleased with the results. They had every reason to give her more work if they wanted to. It was odd, of course, that they had approached her at all. She would have expected a case as sensitive as this to be handled by their regular media management service, whoever they were. Darace's, probably, or Vellochic. But maybe something had gone wrong with that relationship. Maybe Galen were looking to change their chief provider. To Isis? Now wouldn't that be interesting.

There was a soft beep from her vid and a face appeared bottom right, a face she didn't recognise for a moment, round and smooth and framed with long dark hair, a healthy country bloom to the cheeks.

"Hello, Lavendar. This is only a recording so we can't talk. Just to let you know that everything here's fine and that we're thinking about you down there in the big city. I had a message from mother this morning. She said to tell you that Dad's well, a box of birds, as he would say, and that they'll be in touch as soon as they get to Padua. Bye, now!"

Cynthia! So soon. She stood up, smiled, stretched her limbs and realised how long she had been sitting. She had a couple of hours before her dinner date with Curtis Caid. Plenty of time to walk home and change. Except that would hardly be relaxing. A visit to Gloria Bolton, perhaps. A facial and a massage and a new dress. She deserved a little pampering, after all.

5

The Future is in Your Hands!

Vote
ZIG
for
Zero Intervention Government

Free Market!
Free Choice!
Free Speech!
Free World!

Campaign Poster

Spit felt slick with eighty shiners in his pocket (seventy-three after he'd dropped for his shuttle ticket). Dressed in a suit like a smart young gung, red plastic rose in his button-hole, but didn't wear a tie, jack. That was touch. That was delicate, his own move, own man. And sitting cool, beside the window, watching the sliding lights of the city and the dark night sky.

Going down to Nicholson was a freaky business, always a gamble when you crossed your borough boundaries, out into the swamp where you couldn't use your card. But then Spit didn't have a card, not any more. Two days gone and he still hadn't told them. Every day he waited the welfare butchers would do him harder with their questions and their penalties. And every day meant he didn't exist, in some sense, or he existed where his card was and nobody knew. It was real bad biz, jack, but there was a tingle in it too. The ultimate disguise, an ASP forever, because without a card he was nobody and nobody was free. And he felt like he was proving it, riding here on the out-train, first class, with all the slick, rich solos heading for a night in the sin city; most of them hardly looked at him, like he was one of them, except to give him an interested glance or two. Because he had touch maybe. The suit and the rose (an extra point for the rose). And it was all right, jack. It was good. And he could handle it and get away with it. He felt he'd get away with it.

He got out at the Colosseum, along with the rest of them, merged into the crowd milling in the station forecourt, was swept into a current through a high entranceway of shiny black marble. Bigger than he'd ever been in. But it was sweet with the express elevators leaving every few seconds for the higher floors. He crammed in with a bunch of solo stiffs, took it to the twentieth, an empty lobby. There was an escalator going down to the floors below. Twenty minus two, jack. Slick.

Eighteen was a high touch place that freaked him for a minute. A huge spread of space in all directions, soft light, shiny cream floor. Here and there were glass shafts coming out of the ceiling with elevators going up and down. At the bottom of each was a little glass reception with a class-looking slink behind a desk. Spit knew about these places, seen them on TV in the lifestyle programmes. Every elevator went up to a wristic boutique or plutostore on the floor above. There were no big signs, only those little tiny name plates on the door that you couldn't find unless you were told. Nobody ever got past the desk unless they had the clink and heavy with it.

A real touch situation this one, and to prove it there was a lot less people with a lot more flash and velvet and styled-out hair on both sexes. They all walked tall like they owned the joint. Maybe they did. On the other hand, though, maybe they were all on welfare, jack, lost their cards and feeling free and wandering. No. But the thought gave him a kick, a stab of courage, Vacuum. And he squared his shoulders, held his head high, and set off across the cream ice like he had every right to be there. Which he did, jack, shit yes! A was for Attitude, attitude success.

Candy's wasn't hard to find; a long wall with a line of art vids, swirling patterns in soft class colours. The entranceway was a rounded arch with the name in lights above it. Walk in like he belonged. A lobby with a couple of butchers. They were big butchers, dark-skinned, and they had tight white shirts on, silk shirts maybe and so tight they stretched smooth over, moving with the muscles and cuts and rips like a skin. The nipples sticking out like little knobs.

"Good evening, sir," said the one on the right with a white smile. What the shit to do, jack?

"Hi," Spit gave his best smile back, the protean grin of confidence. "I'm here to meet a friend. Mr Blyss."

"I'm not sure I know the gentleman, sir." A sad expression and the muscles seemed to swell even bigger.

This was a situation, jack. OTL. On the line. But the answer was obvious. Clink. It was all about clink. And touch. Spit held out his hand with a twenty dollar piece in it.

"Thank you so much for that information," he said.

"No trouble at all, sir." The dud took the coin, didn't even look at it. His hands went behind his back and his chest rippled like a bag full of snakes. Spit walked on in. Twenty, jack? Shit, he hoped the drinks were cheap.

A glass door slid open and there was music. Guitars, Hawaiian style. And warm air, soft, and trees; there were palm trees all over and a sky above them, a night sky, evening sky with the colour there down low on the horizon still a faint glow of orange.

"Aloha," someone said. A slink in a grass skirt, bare brown belly. She put a rope of flowers round his neck that smelt sweet, sickly, even had a head to it, a buzz like a very special flower.

"Hi," he said.

She waved him through with a floating hand. He was on a wide terrace and there were little tables all around with duds sitting in the twilight. Over to his left, where the music was, a bright lit area with dancers swaying. To the right, a bar busy with waiters. And the sky above him, stars, like it went on forever. Water, he could hear water, the lap of waves. It was the sea.

At the edge of the terrace, there were wide steps going down and a strip of grass there with all the palm trees growing. And then the sand and the waves coming in making little lapping noises, just a white little touch at the edge of them. And out across the water (he could see it better now) the orange line of sky, glowing with the sun gone down, a last faint breath, and a boat there. Yes, it was a boat, a slow-moving cluster of little yellow lights across the bay.

Spit turned, sat down at a table where he could watch it all and listen to the music and the waves and murmur of voices, laughter all around him. Yes, he thought. I got here, jack. This is me. Commitment the Goal and Attitude Success. And knowing it, his head high; high in his head, without a whiff of sniff to carry him, unless it was the flowers, or the viper breathing cool on his brains.

"Good evening, sir." A waitress carrying a tray.

"Sure is," he said. Like a dumbshit, thick kidoda.

"Could I get you a drink, perhaps?" she went on. "Or something to eat?"

A beer. Or maybe not. What would a dud with touch do here? Would a beer be all right?

"I'll have a gin and tonic," he said.

"Certainly, sir." She smiled and made him feel good. "Oh, and moonrise is eight forty-three tonight."

Was that what she said? He wanted to call her back and talk. But that wouldn't work. He couldn't be here with a slink when Blyss arrived. Or maybe he could. Maybe it would be a good idea. But the thought of Blyss had jumped him suddenly. He looked around at the nearby tables. Ords. They were just ords and solos mostly, talking quietly to each other. It was hard to see exactly what they looked like in the dim light. Faint white of shirt sleeves. Warm. It was quite warm.

He still had the flowers round his neck, the scent floating round him, teasing at his head. They were soft and waxy. Real? They felt sort of real. But then he bit one gently and the petal resisted, pushing back against his teeth. And the scent, that was synth as well. He breathed it in and it spread up through his nose like a numb sleepy feeling. Good for the nerves. Like a drag of fudge.

"Ah, yes, of course." It was Blyss, suddenly there, pulling up a chair, folding himself into it. "How are you, my fine young friend?"

"Hi," Spit said. He had to hold it, hold his own. This dud had given him eighty shiners so it had to be all right. Deep down, though, he felt a touch of freak and he thought again of Tobin dying in the alley and the eye. Blyss knew what was in that box for sure, maybe he even put it there. And that was something not to think about.

"Excellent. That's fine." Blyss gave his big, looping smile. No teeth showing. He never showed any teeth. "We have some business to talk through, don't we?"

"Yes. My card."

"Ah-ha. Now wait a minute." Blyss with a long, wagging finger. "I gave you something of mine. A package. Have you got it?"

"I delivered it."

"No, you didn't. You did no such thing. According to my information, the person who was due to receive it never arrived and another unfortunate was, er, how shall I say, inconvenienced. Right?"

Inconvenienced, jack? The dud was DTM and out.

"So?" Blyss persisted. "Hmmm?" His eyes were wide, popping almost, staring, and the brows above them arched up in curved half circles.

"I tossed it," Spit said. Right there in the garbage at the shuttle station.

"After opening it, of course."

"No."

"Don't be silly, boy. You opened it. Didn't it ever occur to you that it might belong to somebody? That someone might have a use for it?"

"What good was it to anyone?"

"What good's a welfid card to people... well... to people who have been inconvenienced?"

Hey! What is this, jack? But Spit didn't move. Couldn't. With Blyss right there, his watching eyes. And the freak was working in him, deep. An ASP doesn't panic, jack, but, shit, oh, shit, it was a situation. A pisshole situation, even for eighty shiners.

The waitress set the glass in front of him. It had an elbowed straw sticking out and a slice of lemon straddling the rim.

"On my tab," Blyss said. "And bring me a scorpion, if you'd be so kind."

"Certainly, Mr Blyss."

"Ah, and something too for my other friend here. Prancing towards us with such natural grace. A beer, probably." The other friend was fattish with a shiny bald head and a drooping black moustache. He, too, grabbed a chair and dragged it to the table, sat down, breathing hard like he'd just run up a wall. He gave a quick glance at Spit and leaned forward, staring at Blyss. He had small eyes and a little screwed-up mouth like something was going to crawl out of it.

"Who's he then?" he said, waving a finger at Spit. "I thought this was going to be private."

"Let me introduce my friend Arlen," Blyss told him. "He's a spit, aren't you, my boy? A tricky little spit. Gets himself in and out of all sorts of interesting places. Like here for example. Very useful quality that." He turned to the bald man and stared at him hard. "Hmmm?" There was no answer.

Spit took a sip through the straw. The drink was cool and bitter. And a good boot of spirit in it. Never had a gin and tonic before.

"Well, Arlen the Spit," Blyss went on. "I'd like you to meet an associate of mine. Mr Biling. Frank Biling. Frank works for Galen Laboratories."

"No names," Biling said, like he had a freak on.

"Hi, jack," Spit said. Watching it. These duds were both on the weirdo side.

"Now," Blyss said, turning back to Biling. "What's interesting in the world tonight? What's been happening to you?"

"You know what's been happening to me," Biling said.

"You intrigue me."

"I'm bloody well in the way of losing my job. And maybe worse."

"Don't concern yourself, my dear fellow. It's not a problem. A random event, merely."

"Exposure. I'm at risk."

The waitress was there with two drinks on a tray. One was a red thing in a tall glass, the other a handle of beer. Nobody spoke while she set them down and moved away.

"The only question from my point of view is whether or not you still want to be cooperative," Blyss said once she'd gone.

"Do I have a choice?"

"My dear fellow, there's always a choice." Blyss reached out and patted the fat man's shoulder. One of his wristic little pickpocket routines. Spit wondered what Biling would find missing in the morning.

"Just give me the stuff," Biling said, "and let me get out of here."

"Tut, tut, tut, tut, tut." Blyss shook his head and then took a slow sip of his drink. Sat there looking at Biling, grinning his big-loopy grin. It was a stare-out, Spit could see. And he could've slotted twenty on who'd drop first.

"We had a deal," Biling said, looking away. See, jack?

"Of course we did. And you'll get everything your little heart desires. I'd just like you to think things through, though. Dwell on the matter. You'll begin to appreciate all the issues, I'm sure."

"I'm starting to come under pressure," Biling said.

"From whom? The Mole? He's been in touch with you?" Nasty little edge to Blyss's voice this time. Not so friendly. NSF. Spit wondered who the Mole was.

58

Biling didn't answer.

"Please, rest easy, my dear fellow," Blyss told him, all palsy-walsy again. "And have confidence in your friends. You know, your lack of faith pains me, just a little. Saddens me. Truly it does. I mean, what's life without faith? Faith's everything. Isn't that so, Arlen?"

What was this, jack?

"Arlen has faith. Faith enough to come here tonight. Not because he trusted me but because he thought he could handle himself."

Was that it? Maybe it was.

"I mean, he could have absconded with the cash I gave him. Or tried to. But he had confidence and he had sense. You understand me?"

The bald man wiped his shiny dome with a fat hand and sighed. Then he let go, just a bit, like he knew he'd just have to wait for Blyss to take his time. Sat back in his chair, took a pull from his beer.

"And I'm sure he appreciates that I only have two options. One is to end his miserable little existence..." Blyss turned to Spit with a big grin, round eyes. And shit, jack, Spit was moving, on his way. "The other is to give him a job."

What? Job? "What job?"

Blyss laughed, leaning back in his chair and spreading his arms like a gameshow host. "See? That's confidence. He should've run for his life but he didn't. The boy's a winner."

Like there'd been a test somehow, one that Spit hadn't even known about. And he'd passed it, jack. A straight, slick win, a little scammer. Spit's luck, maybe. At least he thought he'd passed it.

"What job?" he said again.

"As a runner for me. Doing what you do best. In here, out there. Under the wire." His hand dived down and up again. "Eight hundred a week. Plus bonuses. Cash in hand."

Eight hundred cash? Holy Vacuum! Cash was worth twice as much as welfare credits.

"I need the card, though. To sign."

"Don't worry about that," Blyss said. "Your card's safe enough. It'll be a sort of security against your wages. Investment, you might say. And what are cards, anyway? The shackles of a clumsy bureaucracy, is it not so?" Blyss smiled. An ever bigger smile. This time the teeth almost did show. "You just do as you're told, my young spit, and you'll never have to thumb the city's plastic again. Okay?"

"So who do you work for?" Spit answered, not wanting to sound too eager, showing his cool, but feeling already the crisp smooth surface of the hundred dollar bills.

"Me? Good Lord, boy. I don't work *for* anybody. But in a general sense, and for the purposes of this exercise, we could probably say that we're working *with* Mr David Livid."

Biling gave a snort. "Don't talk about him. Keep him out of this."

"My dear fellow." Blyss was laughing. "Is he not in one sense the hope for all our futures?"

"Futures? Bullshit!"

"Chaos is opportunity and opportunity is freedom. Is it not so? Hmmm?"

"He stuffed me up, that's all I know."

"Nonsense, nonsense, dear fellow." Blyss turned to Spit and smiled, leaned over, patted him on the shoulder, fingered his lapels. Twiddled with the rose in his buttonhole. "A flower," he said. "I like that. Nice touch."

Suddenly, there was a change in the air, a shift to lightness. There, out over the water, the moon was rising, a slice of silver, arc on the horizon, bright; so bright it almost hurt the eyes.

6

Gloria Bolton

SMOOTH AS A LIE

Solo Magazine fashion ad

Sneaky, sneaky, sneaky. Big fat roller, rolling around. Ratman sees it. Ratman knows. Logs and stats and frogs and fats. See the nasty transactions popping out of a network node. See the node going slow, slow, slow with the roller in there, busy there. Then it's up and rolling, moving on and all the network traffic jammed up, crawling. The first node speeding up again with the monster gone and a second one slowing down as the roller gets there, snuggles in and starts its tricks. So, how to catch him, then? Little bit of code maybe. Itty-bitty program to turn the switches, lock the exits, trap him in there. Maybe.

Ratman drank the coke and sat. Scratch. Scratch in the beard where the itchies were, scratch in the groin in the sweaty bit. Think, think, think, though. Because there were could-bes, nasty could-bes. Could be there was more than one. Two, three, four copies of the same roller, up and about there, doing their stuff. Could be it could tell if you were after it, copied itself then just to be sure. Could be there was a master somewhere hidden on disc and waiting for a wake-up call. Had to search the network, all of it, for that. And take forever. Had to track it down, though. Had to get a look inside. So had to talk to Cool Eyes.

"Yes?" She was sitting at a desk in a big window office. Blonde hair, pale skin, statue. City lights behind her. Night then?

"Virus," said the Ratman.

"A virus?"

"Roller."

"What's that?"

Told her. Told her quickly. Nearly didn't stut-tut-tutter one little bit.

"Where are you?" she asked when it was done.

Where?

"95, BG 6, Crossing T-t-t-t...

"Crossing Tower, that's on Willis, right?"

"Right."

"Okay. You want access and I need you here for that. Fifty-second floor, Wakefield Business Centre."

Out? That's scary. Ratman out in the Big Goodbye.

"Why?"

"Because I don't like giving unrestricted access to people I've never met."

"Nothing to w-wear," said the Ratman.

Cool Eyes laughed. Oh, yes. A lovely laugh. The Ratman made her. Wow!

"Okay," Ratman said.

"When can you get here?"

"Fifteen."

"Make it forty-five. Take a shower." Her image faded.

Bitch, to saȳ that. Nasty, nasty. But the laugh was, oh! The Ratman couldn't bear to think of it.

◊

The restaurant had a touch of opulence, heaviness. All velvet drapes, low lights and gleaming silver. And a discreet little table tucked away in a corner. Had Curtis chosen it specially? A tête à tête? Lavendar sipped her Bloody Mary and wondered if he wasn't being just a little bit presumptuous. But that was all right. She felt comfortable, pleased with her day, and pleased too with her new Gloria Bolton in such a setting. Black made its own dark statement and showed off the paleness of her complexion. She was glad that she'd also thought to have the hair styled into something more severe, a little less wild woman.

Curtis was drinking a manhattan and telling her all about his new religion, something put together for him by Deeply Personal Design. It was a kind of sun worship which involved special prayers at set times of the day and a secret morning ritual which was supposed to keep him in tune with the rhythm of the solar system. And perhaps it did. She liked the energy and enthusiasm with which he described it. So important that a person had something to believe in.

"I always thought religion should involve a mystical state, a kind of ecstasy," she said. "Shouldn't ecstasy be the key to it all?"

"I'm not so sure. I considered it, of course. They have special techniques for it, all to do with internal auto-manipulation of various glands. It seemed to me, though, that the whole point of a faith is that you have to work at it. Ecstasy's a possibility in the rites I've got but it doesn't come easily."

She was impressed with this touch of self-denial. Not everyone would feel the need to work for something when you could get it without. Did it show inner depths perhaps?

"Of course," he went on, "I can always add features like that later on if I like. That's the beauty of this new approach. It's all so modular."

Lavendar smiled. She wasn't all that fond of conversations about religion. Such a personal thing, really. Like underwear. She wondered if Cynthia was religious, given that she couldn't have babies and wanted them so much. Perhaps she had beliefs which helped her overcome that disappointment, gave her that inner strength and wisdom. If so, she would be the only one in the family who did believe. Lavendar could imagine what Daddy would say to Curtis's little rituals. 'Load of old cods, if you ask me.' Something like that.

"So, what do you do exactly," she said. "Workwise, I mean."

"Do? I do what I'm told." He laughed. "No, no. I guess I'm a sort of trouble shooter."

"And you work closely with Edmond Eliades?"

"Closely, yes. My actual boss is Carol Carlion, his Financial and Economic Assistant."

Disappointing. But perhaps no more than she might have expected. At their first meeting a few days ago, he had given her the distinct impression that he was Eliades's secretary. Now, it seemed he was merely a dogsbody to an adviser, a lower underling of some kind. He was nice, of course, good company even, and probably he still offered plenty of potential, but it rankled just a little that she had been lied to…well, exaggerated to. Why did people feel the need to do that?

"So, you work in finance yourself?" she asked.

"Usually. Whatever's needed really. I mean, Carol's a genius. She has this absolutely uncanny knack of knowing where the next problem's coming from."

"Oh, and where's that?"

"You mean, now?"

"For example."

"Well, I shouldn't tell you this, really, but we're going to have a very close look at the city's financial systems."

"For the Combined Council?"

"No, no. This is unofficial. Off the record."

Interesting, Lavendar thought. There had been stories for a while that some of the networks were not performing as they should. Perhaps there would be opportunities for an enterprising image management company in a situation like that, especially one that had clients the size of Galen Corporation.

"It's a political issue, of course," Curtis said. "A question of efficiency. I mean, you think about it. Who actually runs this city?"

"Well, the councils are supposed to but…"

"Who does the actual work?"

"The corporations, of course. The Big Three."

"Exactly. Look at Port Nicholson. Eliades Corporation runs the welfare and the tax system. Minerva, also owned by Eliades, handles education. So Eliades collects the tax and pays it to the council, which then pays Eliades for the education and welfare services. I mean, what added value do we get from having those drongos down at the town hall?"

"Absolutely none," Lavendar said, pleased at the heat with which he expressed himself. "I imagine you're a Delwyn Tanner voter."

"Of course."

She smiled at him.

"You too?" He looked almost surprised.

"Gordan Sapich is a personal friend of mine."

"Fantastic!"

"I expect you'll be at the gala tomorrow."

"No, worse luck. I have to work." He pulled a face, terribly disappointed, poor man.

"That's a pity. It would've been nice to share the fun with someone. But I expect there'll be another time."

"I do hope so."

◊

Grey walls, desk, a round table with six chairs. Ratman sat in one of them and looked out of the window at the lights. Weird, oh, weird. And hairy, scary way up here.

"Coffee?" Cool Eyes asked.

"Y-y-yes."

She had her maker on a low cupboard by the window. Poured a cup for Ratman, one for her. It watched her hands.

"How do you take it?"

"Sugar. Th-th-three."

"So." She sat down opposite, but it didn't, couldn't look. Her eyes. Real eyes, real hair. Real skin. It was all too close, too.... Watch the coffee, Ratman. Eyes down in the cup, now. Boy, oh boy, oh boy.

"The problem I have," she said, "is the motive behind this

thing. You tell me it's a virus and yet it's doing stuff that looks like fraud. So, is it put there for that purpose? Is it designed to carry out a specific set of actions that will benefit somebody?"

"D-don't know."

"How do we find out?"

"C-c-catch it. T-take a look."

"Catch it?"

"M-m-memory dump."

"You want to reverse engineer it."

"Y-yes."

"That sounds like a tough job even for the genius they tell me you are."

Ratman nodded, sipped the coffee. Ratman didn't like it here. And didn't, didn't, didn't. Cool Eyes, looking, saw through, saw in. Eyes like a mirror made the Ratman feel and sense itself and it didn't like it. No, no, no.

"So what are you going to do?"

"G-g-got to track it, number one. Need your network management system. Do something with that."

"What?"

"Don't kn-n-now yet. Got to look. Find out which g-g-gear he likes maybe. Where he goes."

"And then?"

And then and when and when and then. The Ratman couldn't think with Cool Eyes on him, couldn't, couldn't get a handle on it. Watching the coffee, its coffee, her coffee, seeing her fingers curled round the brown mug, pale fingers, slim fingers, touchy, touchy things. If they touched the Ratman it would scream. "And then we try and see where he goes. We try and set up for him. We put a little tweaky in there, d-d-dump him when he doesn't see."

"Tweaky?"

Tweaky, freaky. Ratman watched the fingers, one set round the mug, the other on the table top like they were resting, curled up just a little. Resting, ready to jump.

"Little patch on the OS. M-m-memory management. P-pop the partition."

"So you'll need unrestricted access. All over."

"Master blaster."

"Yes. And that's what bothers me," Cool Eyes said. "I've worked with you folk a couple of times before. It hasn't always been that successful."

Uh-oh. Trouble now.

"It's not that you don't know your stuff. I've got no complaints on that score. It's just that you seem to have a finely judged capacity for annoying people. Customers. Perhaps there's a certain deficiency in social skill. You know what I mean?"

Mean and been and seen and clean. Skill and will and nil and spill. Eyes on your coffee, Ratman. Keep the eyes down there in the clear black down-down. Ratman doesn't hear. Ratman doesn't know.

"How old are you?"

HELP ME!

"T-t-t-t-t-t-t-t-t-t-t..."

"It doesn't matter. It's just that there really isn't anyone who has complete and unrestricted access to this network."

"Except th-th-th-th..."

"Yes. Except the roller." She sighed. "Look, all right, we'll go ahead. I'll just need to keep an eye on you, that's all. You won't mind that, will you?"

Looked at her, then. Looked at her, couldn't help but look at her and she smiled a little, oh so nicely sad little smile, pretty like a movie star. And what can Ratman do?

◊

"And your parents?"

"At the moment they're in Italy," said Lavendar. "My mother's been attending a conference and now they're travelling around. Just taking a holiday. Well, my father's probably working, really. Getting ideas for an article of some kind."

"He's a writer?"

"A journalist, yes. The old-fashioned kind. One word is

worth a thousand pictures." She took another mouthful of venison, a delicate morsel on the end of her fork. Really, it was delicious, succulent, tender but sweet with a high, gamy flavour. She wondered if it had been genetically engineered.

"Might I have read anything of his?" Curtis asked. "In *Solo*, for example?"

"Perhaps. But he mostly publishes overseas. In fact they're hardly ever home these days. "

"Nice to have parents who are independent."

"Oh, indeed. Wouldn't it be awful if one had to look after them. If they were poor." Such an awful word. So degrading for everyone concerned.

"No one to blame but themselves," Curtis said. "A friend of mine's a psychologist and he believes poverty is essentially a neurosis."

"Really?"

"If people were properly motivated, they'd get themselves out of it."

It might be true. Why not? And if it were, then obviously, the city shouldn't be spending all that money on welfare handouts, they should give people counselling instead. She sipped her wine. A pinot noir. Curtis had chosen it well.

"If you're in a bad spot, you just have to fight your way through," he went on.

"A challenge."

"Yes, exactly."

It was a fine word, challenge, a stirring word. And it made her feel proud, just a little, to think of the challenges she'd met in her own life, how far she'd come in the eight years since she enrolled in media management at the university. Sometimes, though, she suspected there might be challenges which were just too big, just too difficult to deal with. She thought of Derek Mountain lying in his hospital bed and what his future might be. A wave of sadness swept through her, a surprising strength of feeling, so that she wondered for a moment if there might not be something wrong with her to be so upset about someone she hardly knew. But that was a silly thought.

Just because she felt sad about what happened to Derek Mountain, didn't mean she had a problem. Not like that friend of Simon's who was a diagnosed pathophiliac and getting treatment for it, always worrying about the unemployed and the downtrodden and were they getting enough to eat.

"I suppose you could say that the poor are economically challenged," she said.

"That's it. That's it exactly." Curtis was beaming at her. "You know," he said, "You're one hell of a lady!"

Lavendar smiled, mostly to herself. Curtis would almost certainly want to make love to her. But would that be appropriate? Not on their first date, obviously. But later? Would she come to like him that much? And how much did you need to like somebody? It seemed a kind of joke, a riddle. She smiled again and realised, suddenly, that Curtis thought her expression was all for him.

7

How well do you score?

Here's our typical reader profile. Do you match up?
- Age 25 to 40
- $500,000 plus salary
- Tertiary education
- Single
- No kids (God forbid!)
- Lives within sight of the harbour
- Eats out 5 nights a week
- Votes ZIG
- Shops at Cardoman, Dead Rep and Gloria Bolton
- Listens to Musky Jack and the Lyrix
- Has never read Samantha Cole or Draper Bacon
- Goes raving and indoor skiing
- Hates Banjax
- Sexual preferences? (none of your business)

Solo Magazine

The room was down in the basement of the Colosseum, one of a thousand doors in a maze of blank concrete corridors. Inside, though, it had touch. It was class decor, jack. Fat leather furniture and art vids on the walls and drapes and soft lights.

"Welcome!" Blyss said, closing the door behind him. "Do sit down."

Spit slid himself into the corner of a squodgy sofa.

"I think we should seal our bargain, eh?" The same wristic, loopy grin. "Let's celebrate, my boy. How about a drink?"

"Sure," Spit said. "Okay."

Blyss opened a cupboard in the wall: glass shelves with glasses on them, a mirror behind, all gleaming bright.

"Tonight a celebration and a special treat. Tomorrow we work." Blyss had his back turned, was talking over his shoulder.

"Do you live here, jack?"

"Live? Now, that's an interesting word. Does anybody live, my friend? That's a very good question." He turned round, holding two small glasses full of pale, violet liquid. "Here, then. Let's drink to this most fortunate day."

Sure, jack, why not? Spit held the glass to his mouth and it gave off a little gust of fumes, aniseed and alcohol and something else. His lips felt scared of it, suddenly.

"What's this?" he asked.

"It's brainjoy. Good for the soul. Gives it a bang, so to speak." Blyss lifted the glass and, with a quick jerk of his head, threw the contents back into his throat. Then he grinned, laughed, nodded with round, popping eyes. Oh, shit, Spit thought. Let's do it, jack. Give it a try. V for victory and Sha-Ka-Bla.

The liquid hit his mouth like a sweet sticky smear and slid down his gullet, he could feel it falling, and then, suddenly, it was alive, hot, twisting, leaping at him, coming up again in a gust of fumes that exploded into the back of his nose, his head. It was in his brain, jack, he could feel it clawing through his skull to the outside, cold on his scalp; and his eyes, he could see things, stars and shapes and strange sounds. He could see the sounds. They were whirling in his head.

"Good, good," said Blyss, and the words were like stars bursting, flash, flash, and falling fire. "And now a little treat, my boy. Let me give you a special treat."

Blyss looming over him suddenly, taking his arm. Spit stood up, swaying, his brain and vision yawed, but it wasn't sick, not a sick feeling. Cool, jack, touch of cool, like he was open, soft inside.

The door, a corridor, the light went on and the narrow

passage focused down its empty length to another door at the far end.

"Go on now, my boy." Blyss's fingers on his shoulders, touching him, patting at him, bony things like lizards, dancing lizards, laughing. Who was laughing, jack? Spit. It was Spit and the thin man laughing at the squeezing lizard things. And laughter dancing, leaping like a bunch of stripped slinks. But not slinks, no. They were shapes of light and shadow, bits of flit and happy purposes.

Door opening into a square room, sofa in the middle, a big sofa, enormous, rolling arms and back like waves of comfort turning outwards, breaking like the sea. And the walls shiny, dark black glass, reflections, Spit and Blyss dim and creeping across the floor like sneakies.

He sat, and his brain came down a bit. He got his focus, noticed he was laughing; feeling sad though too, a strange slow sadness, pity, jack, because the sounds were gone. He couldn't see them any more, only the things, like the ghosts in the shining walls and Blyss's pale face, a floating head, all pale and bony, loopy grin.

Flick, and the room exploded. It was twice as big, the walls were pictures, image of a great hall hung with drapes of rich red, purple, gold and statues, stone pale naked figures, light of torches dancing. People. There were people coming down among the arches, three of them. And one was stripped, a young dud, white like the statues but with golden hair and, on either side of him, a pair of guards in black-brown leather, butchers, gleam of metal studs.

Someone was laughing. Spit turned, looking for Blyss, but the room was empty now except for the living walls. And there in the great hall, sweeping across the floor in a gown of white, was a fat slink with long red hair tied back in a golden braid. Her white face, round like the moon with red lips, laughing, chins all shaking. She was huge and looming in the wall, her little eyes like pearls, her huge tits rolling like a wave, coming on so fast that Spit cringed back, afraid she'd swamp him. Shit, jack. Turned his eyes away.

There, where the guards were. They had the stripped dud tied, his wrists bound with a strap, his arms above his head, a chain which hauled them up towards the ceiling. Standing there and the fat slink surging down on him, her arms wide, mass of body draped in acres, floating white. She was still laughing. She embraced him from behind, hugging him, smothering him with kisses across his neck and shoulders, so much happy laughter as she let him go and stepped away, just for a moment.

Another flick in the walls. The big view of the hall had gone and there were different screens now, each an angle on the same scene; the blond dud's face, his smooth white back, the fat slink's face, a long shot of the two of them standing there. Her hands began to stroke the white flesh down his sides. Her red nails, long and pointed sharp, like killers. She smoothed him, crooned to him. He smiled with his eyes closed. She was staring full at Spit, a big smile creased across her moon face, moon.

"Good boy, oh, my good sweet boy." Like Blyss's voice, her big hands, fat with fingers, rings of gold and the long nails. Laughing face. Slowly, delicately, she drew the red claws across the white skin.

"Lovely boy," said the moon. "I want to eat you, don't I?"

Dud with his eyes closed, quivering, his lips apart and the nails stroked lightly, little points drew soft indented lines.

"Spit," said the face and Spit was ripped with sudden terror. "Spit, my lovely boy!" The white eyes round and laughing. Voice was shouting. "Bouncy! Bouncy! Bouncy!" And the nails dug deep into the white flesh, dragging, slicing blood, and the blond dud screamed and Spit was screaming with him, curled up tight in a corner of the sofa, screaming as the fear ripped down, the nails tearing deep inside him, jack, so deep he never knew the end, it wouldn't stop.

But then it did stop, panting there, his eyes closed, image in his brain of the face and the nails and the White Rabbit's cry and a strange, happy feeling that he was still there, still alive. And after a while, he began to feel the world outside his head where the sounds had stopped and nothing moved. He opened his eyes, and moved his arms. And then Blyss was standing over him saying, "There, my boy, there's your treat, now. You liked that, didn't you? Come on, wake up, now. Time to go home."

PART TWO

livid

8

YOU are there

Feel the excitement of the French Revolution.

Have tea with your favourite movie star.

**Dive the Great Barrier Reef with
the Partner of Your Dreams.**

Startech Productions launches an all new wave
of Remote Audio Visual Experience like nothing
you've ever known on Earth.

RAVE
the New Wave!

BE THERE! HAVE IT ALL!

Shuttle Station Ad

In the little grey meeting cubicle, Lavendar logged her call to Dougall Myerson and waited. Her ghost, dark haired this morning, stared back at her from the glass curve of the vid wall. Across the middle of its forehead, her id glowed red. Today, she thought, in a few moments, everything might change. If Myerson liked what she had done with Carl Robollo's media releases, if he decided to give Isis more work, if.... She hardly dared think what it might mean in case it didn't happen. Stay calm, she told herself. Don't want it too much. But, then, why not? The more you wanted the more you got, surely.

The vid wall lit up and the little desk in front of her had

suddenly become part of a table, three-sided, with two other people sitting at it. On her right was Myerson, on her left Robollo. Only a faint seam between them showed they were not actually in the same room but in separate cubicles of their own.

"Good morning," Dougall said.

"Hello," she answered, smiling.

Carl said nothing. His presence there was a good sign, though. It must be.

"And thanks for yesterday," Dougall went on. "We released the material you developed and it seems to be holding. Wouldn't you say, Carl?"

"Yes," Robollo cleared his throat. "Yes, it's all right so far."

"And how's the patient?" she asked.

"The same. Induced catatonic psychosis is the medical term for it."

"Is he going to be okay?"

"We don't know. We're anticipating, though, that whatever happens there's going to be an investigation."

"Something, perhaps, you can help us with," Robollo said.

Yes, then! They did want her!

"We'd like to be in a position where we don't actually have to face any surprises when the investigation starts," Dougall said.

"How can I help?"

"Carl?"

Robollo cleared his throat again. "Well," he said. "We have security videos all through the labs, of course. And we have some play of this particular incident. Here, take a look..."

A window opened in the top middle of the vid. It showed a small room with white walls. To the left was a computer workstation. In the centre stood a chair, heavily padded, with adjustable foot and head rests. Attached to the side of it, below the right arm, was a little shelf which held a black helmet with a milky white visor. Three cables, red, white and yellow, ran from the top of the helmet, connecting it to sockets in the chair.

After a few seconds, a man and a woman wearing white lab

coats came into the room. The woman went over and sat down at the workstation and read figures from the screen while the man made adjustments to the helmet and cables.

"These are the technicians, Frank Biling and Hillary Bowdendale," Dougall said. "Frank's one of our supervisors."

"What does this test actually do?" Lavendar asked.

"It looks at neural activity in the cerebral cortex and translates it into higher level, more meaningful patterns," Carl told her.

"It reads your mind?"

"Nothing so dramatic. Although we can often recover images and sounds which seem to make sense to the patient. No, it's really an advanced form of EEG, only more targeted and easier to interpret. More accurate in its diagnostic capabilities."

The patient, Derek Mountain, arrived in a wheelchair pushed by an orderly. He was young, maybe thirty years old, with close cropped blond hair and a long, bony nose. He was wearing a green hospital gown with a blue rug or blanket over his knees. His hands lay slack in his lap and as he came in he looked round the room with a slow lolloping turn of his head.

"What's wrong with him?" Lavendar asked.

"He's under sedation. He came into Ward 27 with severe muscle spasms in his right leg. We judged it was stress related," Myerson answered.

"We were giving him this test as part of a program to target his medication as closely as possible," Robollo added.

"What does he do?"

"He's a systems engineer."

Slowly, leaning on the orderly's arm, Mountain stood up and moved into the testing chair. Biling made sure he was comfortable and then picked up the black helmet and fitted it over his head. He and Hillary exchanged some words about the test settings and Biling adjusted the cables again. The orderly pushed the wheelchair into a corner and left the room.

A second window opened up on Lavendar's wall vid. It showed a block of graphs; each had its own independent worm wavering gently, indicating variations in the equipment somewhere. She guessed it was the monitoring information from Hillary's screen and that the graphs were indicating something about Derek's brain patterns. She ignored them and concentrated on the image of the room with the chair and the patient and Biling standing next to them with his arms folded. Nothing seemed to be happening. The only movement was the little red counter in the corner of the window, ticking over the seconds.

"Everything normal here?" Dougall Myerson asked.

"Yes," Carl told him. "All channels functioning."

Derek seemed relaxed, arms resting along the arms of the chair, his hands curled into loose fists. Knees together.

"Now," Carl said. "Watch this."

Suddenly, one of the graphs on Hillary's computer screen went haywire, leaping and wriggling like a frantic snake.

"That's channel 94. High visual feedback. Now watch 98, the audio."

Another worm went crazy.

Hillary's voice came from out of shot, alarmed. "It's thrashing." Derek Mountain's hands tensed suddenly and his forearms and legs started to shake. Frank Biling, however, didn't move. Just stood there still with his arms folded, watching.

A third graph went out of control.

"Channel 56. One of the tactiles," Robollo said.

"Frank!" Hillary shouted. Biling looked up, stared at her in surprise.

"Thrashing on three channels!" she said. "Four now."

A painful pause. The seconds ticked over.

"All right," Biling said. "Kill it! Kill it!"

Hillary started to talk instructions into her machine, trying to keep her voice calm so that she wouldn't be misunderstood. Slowly, one by one, the worms settled down. Derek Mountain sat, slumped to one side, unconscious. Biling was on the phone, calling for help.

The windows disappeared. Lavendar found both men staring at her.

"You can see the problem," Myerson said.

Yes, she could certainly see the problem. Any newso who got a look at this clip would want to know why Frank Biling took fifteen seconds to respond to an obvious crisis.

"What do you suggest?" Dougall asked.

Suggest? What were they asking? That she doctor a security tape. Yes, well, of course she could do that but....

"So what happened?" she asked. "Did he explain?"

"He panicked. It was the first time he'd supervised an ENAS."

"This used to be a category A test," Carl Robollo said. "Qualified medical supervision only. We recently downgraded it to B, Technical Supervisor."

"Even if we threw Biling to the wolves it wouldn't help us much," Myerson said.

"Hardly the decent thing to do," Robollo added. "And, anyway, he might talk. Better to save his bacon."

By doctoring a security tape and misleading an investigation?

"So." Myerson stared at her.

"What about Hillary?" Lavendar asked. "Maybe she wouldn't cooperate."

"I guess she'd have to be persuaded. Off the record, of course."

"Getting her on side would have to be part of the deal." Robollo said.

◊

"Arlen? Is that you?"

Who else would it be, jack? Spit, with excitement, all the thrill of his new life singing in him, just wanted to run, get out of there, pretend he hadn't heard. He was too slow, though. The second voice caught him.

"Arlen! Come here, boy!"

Sitting in the kitchen, the Farter jammed up in the corner with his belly pressed tight against the table top, the Muddler with her back to the door, turning, peering over her shoulder. The two of them, one fat, one thin. Books and papers spread around them, pissarse studies, SKB. And not for Spit no more. No, jack, not any more. His spirit leapt again at the thought of it.

"Where've you been, boy?" his father asked.

Spit took a few steps into the room but not too far, jack, hovered in the narrow space between the cupboards and the sink bench.

"Haven't seen you for ages, seems like," his mother said, smiling. A drag-down sort of smile, pathetic bony face. Like she expected no-one to ever take any notice of her, which nobody did much. Except the Farter and Spit, occasionally. Spit hated it when she smiled like that.

"One day you're sick in bed, the next you're gone from dawn to, well, who knows when you came in last night? Have a good time?" The Farter was leaning forward, forearms resting plump across the books. There was a big grey stain of sweat on the front of his T-shirt. Hot in the room. The central heating on for once.

"I expect he had a good time," his mother said. "I expect he was down at the Community Hall with the other young people."

Spit remembered Candy's and the glass of brainjoy, the strange image of the fat white woman who called him by his name. He didn't understand the way that had slammed him, watching those red nails rake down, white skin dragged in bleeding lines. The young dud's back like a ploughed field, if he'd ever seen one; put the seeds in there, jack. Weird, a freaky piece. And if he were a true ASP, free of all the fuck-shit sense of right and wrong, then maybe he could do that too, just drag his own nails, sharpened, down a wrister's back and make him scream. The proof of power, the attitude.

"Arlen?" the Muddler said. "Are you all right?"

Tell them, Spit thought. Cough the snot, jack, CTS.

"I got a job," he said.

"What?"

"Job?"

The pair of them, their eyes round and wide, like four glass marbles ready to drop out and roll over the pissing floor.

"What sort of job?" the Farter asked.

"Working for a company downtown. David Livid Enterprises."

"Doing what?"

"Errands. Messages."

"You need a bloody degree to get a job running messages!"

"Not at this place. They want somebody quick. And clever."

"Not illegal, is it?"

"No, dear," the Muddler said. "It wouldn't be illegal. Arlen would never do anything illegal. Would you, dear?"

"Nagh!" Spit said, to keep them sweet. And who cared? ASP for ever, free and easy, jack. His own boss. Seize the day!

"Sounds fishy to me," the Farter said.

"I expect it's all right," the Muddler told him.

"Doesn't make sense, though." Stumpy hand in the thinning grey hair, eyes with that puzzled look, like he was going to cry.

"He's a clever boy, Clive. We always said he was a clever boy."

"But I can't get a job running messages and look at all the work I've put in. All these years." He looked down at the books. Whatever they were. *Introductory Concepts in Elementary Cost Accounting* was the title on one of them. Big letters. So it was easy to read, maybe. All that shit kidoda. Tell them, Spit thought. Wristic pisshole.

"It's no good, jack. Reading that crap. You've got to get out and find it. Got to slam for it."

"Oh, Arlen!" The Muddler staring at him in disappointment. Reproach, that was the word.

"Where's your respect?" the Farter demanded, little squeak. He was in a blaze, as close as he ever got to one.

Too much slam for the Muddler, though. "Oh, but he respects you, Clive. I'm sure he does."

"I'm not talking about me. I'm talking about the system we have here. Best for everyone. It gives us all a chance, doesn't it? Helps us to improve ourselves. Not like being tossed on the scrap-heap. No, sir."

"Gobbling junk that nobody wants?" Spit said.

"There's a big shortage of cost accountants. It was on the news. Anyway, you can't expect to be getting welfare for nothing. Wouldn't be right."

"That's true, dear." The Muddler nodding.

"So how much does this job pay you?" The Farter changing tack.

"Three hundred a week. Cash." Tell them more and they'd be charging him board.

"Well, bugger me."

"Clive! Language, dear!"

"Well, bugger me, I repeat. That's more than the benefit in real money. That's a real job."

"Yes, he said it was."

"I don't know. I can't figure it out. I mean, I've done my duty, haven't I? A faithful servant. Twenty years I've been on the books in this borough, doing the best I could. I've never missed a retraining assignment in all that time, you know that? Everything. Welding? I nearly burnt my thumb off with that welding course. Remember that?"

"Oh, yes, dear. That was a bad time."

And that was it. Enough. Spit had had enough. "I gotta go," he said, turning, heading for freedom.

"Take care, boy!" The Farter calling after him.

And down the hall and through the door. OMW. On my way, jack. All action eager, full of slam and bounce. Didn't bother with the lift even but ran the stairs, down seven flights, in round and round, swinging round the corners on the rail, where there was a rail, and ploughing through the papers and the crap and dirty cartons, beer cans, the plastic wrappings, rat-mouse rustle, down.

And boom! Out into the day, the blue sky bright above

him, brilliant blue, and left it all behind him, the geri whinging, whining gees. All that pissing gratitude.

He breathed in the air. Yes. Freedom. F for freedom. Clink in his pocket, jack, and promise on the way. Today he had to make his first call. Shuttle into Nicholson and then downtown. Blyss had an office in a building off Johnston Street. Easy biz for a mover, jack. And afterwards, he'd have his hair touched. A decent touch with slick down the sides. And maybe think about a new suit, a superfibe or polysynx. He had it, jack. He had it all.

> V was for Victory and out of the mess
> A was for Aptitude, got it for everything
> C was for Confidence, of course he could do it
> U was for...

He couldn't think of a new U for the moment and didn't give a shit. New U, jack? It's a new me! And he laughed at the sky.

9

Fee's Love Nest

There's some curious goings-on in a penthouse down in Thorndon. Recently bought by Fabulous Fiona Duncannen, the darling of the Rich and Beautiful, the 400 square metre luxury pad has been the scene of several interesting little tête-à-têtes in the last few days. *Pump Trend* has it on good authority that the lovely Fee may be more than a fraction intimate with latest boy-friend Saigo Bruce. 'I've seen them several times,' our informant told us. 'And they were being very friendly.' Sly Saigo's business manager, Robyn Vinon, refused to comment but we're convinced that romance is in the air. Now, what will Daddy say, Fiona?

Pump Trend

Ratman, Ratman. Goggle-eyed inside the headset. Staring, staring, eyeballs smeared with Optigene to stop them drying out. The sound, the images, the data in so fast it didn't dare to blink. For this was high-power mode, the mainliner. Charlie Cato firing down the problems back to back and Ratman catching them and doing them, returning them so quick that Charlie found it hard to hold the pace. A debug, a surocode design, a nasty little number with a fourth dimension. Ratman cracked em, stacked em, packed em. Always asking more, more, more. A hungry Ratman, couldn't get enough when it was going like this, the addict Ratman, drain brain sucking. Didn't care now about the other guys, didn't care now about the nodes out there, the friends of seven years. The Ratman on the fix was pumping blood and ecstasy.

– Well, Charlie said at last. That's about it.
– No, Charlie. No, Charlie. Please.
– You better take it easy, boy. Too much of this stuff's not good for you.
– Ratman doesn't care. Ratman take it. Ratman want it bad, bad, bad.
– Sorry, son. I can't do that.
– Pleeeeeeeeeaaaase!
– I got a problem you can generate some ideas on, though. Non-specific situation.
– What's that, Charlie?
– Going into the hard. The neural physical connection?
– Thinking on a wire, Charlie? That's impossible.
– Maybe not. I got some research here from MIT and a theory. Also a guy from down your way has some ideas about Feynmann tunnels. Robollo, the name is.
– New to me.
– NPC theory's new to everybody. I'll send it down and you can let me know what you think. Maybe, I can find someone mad enough to give it a try.
– Ratman mad.
– I know you're mad, boy, but I don't want to fuck your head any more than it's done already. You make me too much money. All I want from you's the theory. No silly experiments.
– Gimme, gimme, gimme.
– All in good time. Now, how's that Southern Systems number?
– I got a roller.
– Roller? You been talking to Ramesh then. Over this side we call those things frogs.
– Roly-poly froggy-woggy.
– How you getting on with the customer?
Cool Eyes, oh Cool Eyes, what does poor Ratman do?
– We go good.
– Just make sure you don't upset anybody. I know that lady. I dealt with her before.
– She keep an eye on Ratman, said so.

— I bet she will.

And Charlie gone then. Sending down a bunch of stuff on NPC. And Ratman taking it, unwrapping it, but not so quick now. Lost the edge. And lost the urge. And Cool Eyes watching, pale like a ghost, like an angel, cold and smiling. Ratman running, running through the pine trees, lost in the dark.

◊

Spit Wilson on his fourth job of the day, to and from the office off Johnston Street. It was easy biz, jack, kid easy. Sometimes he took messages to Blyss, other times he took messages away and delivered them to duds around Port Nick. He had his own cell phone and a special carry for the job, a little rig with a slot that took the dataslices. It was attached to his wrist by a radex cord, a safety device, Blyss told him, which would yank loose and erase the memory of the slice if anyone tried to grab it and run. Weren't no duds about to do that, though. Not the way Spit figged it. He was too quick, quick and slick. He was free and skimming, zipping in and out on the shuttle, or up on the tubestreet, diving into strange doors opened by duds he didn't know. They were weird duds, some of them, a bunch of wristic suits or slinks with shades and painted lips. Or down on the street, jack. There were even jobs down there with some smelly bundle like a nonno; except that those duds looked sharp enough, and Spit figged maybe they were in disguise. He thought of Tobin's dead man sometimes, but not too much. Because it was different now. Now he was on the inside, jack. He could tell by the way they treated him. Looking at him with who-the-fuck when he first did the door, but when he said his biz, jack, and showed them the rig, well shit they changed their tune. They couldn't wait to get their codes into the carry and get that data ripped away. It was a strange kind of attention they gave him then, jack, the shift in how they looked. They needed what he had. That was cool. He liked that.

Blyss's office was a square little room close down by the street. It was done out slick with furniture all chrome and black like leather, with a desk and a table and a couple of chairs, a sofa, a door out the back with a flight of steps going down. No windows, only a big wall vid that played drag-arty pictures most of the time. Vids were everywhere in Blyss's world, Spit noticed. Vids, he figged, were Blyss's biz somehow.

This time when he got back, Blyss was sitting on the sofa staring at nothing, just sitting, with his long legs stretched out half across the room. Didn't seem to see when Spit came in, didn't move. Like he was frozen, jack, a real freako. Sitting there statue with a half-drunk cup of coffee in his hands.

"You okay, jack?"

Blyss blinked, gave a twitch of his head.

"Ah, my young friend," he said, smiling, sitting up straight, like Spit had flicked a switch. He put the coffee cup down on a little table and leaned forward with his elbows on his knees. "What have you got for us, then?"

Holding out his hand like it was all normal. Spit released the cord and gave him the carry. Blyss entered his code and pulled out the dataslice. Then he reached into the jacket of his three-piece suit and took out a little reader. He slipped the slice inside and stared at the screen while he checked the contents.

"You could do all that by radio," Spit said. "Or a VRF modem."

"You trying to talk yourself out of a job?" Blyss laughed. "People listen to radios, my boy. And they tap wires. Sometimes the old ways are best."

"But how do you know the people I give those slices to are the ones supposed to get 'em?"

"I hope you take them where you've been instructed!" Blyss said.

"But who's to say the duds at the door are really the ones?"

"The wrong people don't know the entry codes, do they?"

"Maybe they slammed the real customer. Some duds'd crack, jack. Pressure."

Blyss laughed. "Goodness me, boy. You do have an imagination. Whoever do you think we are dealing with here? This is a civilised business community, not some low-life wolf-pit. Although, of course..." He hesitated, seemed to be thinking about something. Then he sighed, like it was all too boring, ho-hum. "It's true, though, that we occasionally have to deal with people in a more forceful way than usual."

"You mean Tobin, right?" With the eye in the box.

"For example."

"Is he the dud who got done in the alley?"

"That was an associate of Mr Tobin's. Dispensable, I'm glad to say."

"Who did him? The Mole?" Spit wasn't sure he wanted to hear the answer.

"That, my friend, is a very good question, indeed. We have our suspicions. We believe it was someone over-reacting and Mr Molle could quite easily be subject to that. Rest assured, though, we shall certainly find out, one way or anther. Mr Livid has ways and means. For now, though, it's certainly nothing you should trouble yourself about. A mere blip in our normal business dealings."

"Sure, jack. Sure."

"Happy, then?" Blyss asked.

◊

"**I** don't understand." Hillary Bowdendale was frowning but Lavendar thought that she understood perfectly well.

"I'm merely suggesting that you shouldn't worry about any repercussions here. I'm sure the official record will show that you and Frank took all the appropriate actions in a very timely fashion."

"Why would the record show that if it wasn't true?"

Lavendar didn't answer. Just smiled her best smile. A little flicker of fear passed over Hillary's face. Nice face really; a little wide in the cheekbones but something could be done with it, if she'd only wanted to try.

"Well, it wouldn't, of course. But who knows what you remember in an emergency? People often report very different versions of traumatic events. When you actually come to look at the record, you may well find it isn't as you remembered."

"I don't like it," Hillary said and there was no reason why she should, was there? Just an honest young woman, trying to do her job, trying to make her way in the world. Quite admirable in her rectitude when you came to think about it.

"Look," Lavender told her, "it's not a problem. All I'm really saying is that the security video of the test will be released as part of any investigation and that it might be a good idea if you took a look at it ahead of time."

"Is that all you're saying?"

"Of course."

"Well, yes. I certainly will check. It's only sensible."

"Good. I'm quite sure that whatever you want to say will be borne out by the record."

When Hillary had gone, she started up the on-line media editor and loaded the play from the ENAS test, and wondered what she could do with so little to work with. Stripping off the timer numbers was easy, as was cutting out ten seconds of Frank Biling's inactivity. The difficulties came with the visual graphical displays off Hillary's computer screen. It just didn't seem possible to find two precise moments where all the wriggling worms were aligned in a manner which allowed her to make a cut. She tried two, three, five, six cuts, with tinier, tinier splices, but in every case, even to an untrained eye, it was obvious that the graphical output was discontinuous on at least one of the channels. In the end, she had to resort to actually redrawing small sections of two of the graphs at a point where the others could be closely aligned. Something like. It looked good, at least, although, of course, she had no idea whether or not it made sense to anyone who understood the movement on the displays.

Finally, she had to deal with the voices. She took a single sentence out of the conversation she had just had with Hillary and tweaked the tone and intonation just a fraction. Then she did the same thing with some of the words off the play, rearranged everything and put it all back together again.

The final result was fine, yes, nice. She sat back and watched it, smiling to herself. Pleased. And why not?

First the channel 94 worm went crazy and, almost immediately, channel 98 as well.

"Frank!" Hillary called, not puzzled or panic stricken but nicely urgent.

Biling turned to her at once.

"I don't like it," Hillary said.

Right on cue, channel 56 started doing its stuff.

"It's thrashing," Hillary called.

"All right, kill it! Kill it!" Biling decisive, urgent.

It had all taken just four and a half seconds in the little red timer numbers. Such responsiveness, such concern for the poor patient, who only visibly tensed for the shortest possible moment of time. Hillary and Frank could be proud of themselves watching this.

She saved the original play, just in case she should need it again, you never knew. Then she sent the new one back to Myerson along with a copy of her conversation with Hillary, for his information. So, customer satisfied. Problem solved.

Except that now she'd finished and the self-absorption of the work was over, the doubts began to creep in. Had she done the right thing? Should she have taken the job at all? It was not so much the moral issue, the fact that the doctored security tape might mislead an investigation; that, after all, was Galen's responsibility. She'd only done what the customer wanted, and the customer was always right, of course. No, her misgivings came from a sense that something was just a little awry with the situation, that Myerson and Robollo were not being entirely honest with her. Why had the test gone wrong? If overloading was the reason, why had Frank Biling been so slow? The memory of his standing there while poor Derek Mountain twitched and writhed made her feel very uncomfortable. It didn't look like panic, more like... She didn't know.

A blink on her screen. A window opened with Simon's face.

"A couple of calls while you were busy," he said. "One was a bit weird."

"Why?"

"A woman, wouldn't give her name, but seemed to know you. Old."

"Old?"

"Well, oldish. Bit of a down-sider, I'd say. Respectable enough but, well, you know. Big Parade Fashions? And second hand?"

Could it be? No, it couldn't be. It couldn't. Impossible.

"What did she want?" Lavendar asked.

"Just to talk, she said. I saved the message if you want to..."

"No! I don't have time for that. I don't want to listen to those kind of messages. Please program the system so that person never gets through here again." But if she didn't want to look, didn't that mean she really thought....

"Are you all right," Simon asked.

"I'm fine!" Snappy. She shouldn't snap at Simon, it wasn't his fault. She took a deep breath, sighed. "I just hate those sort of calls, that's all." And on top of her doubts about Galen. It wasn't fair.

"Well, here's one you might like better."

A second window opened, big with a huge bunch of yellow flowers, a riot of gold and lemon and orange.

"Good afternoon, Lavendar." It was Curtis's voice. "Thanks for a wonderful evening yesterday. And do enjoy the gala. Sorry I won't be there."

Yes, she thought, yes. That helps a little bit, maybe.

◊

Spit was high and flying like he'd had another whiff of brainjoy, like a long sniff of frosty air. He knew where he was going, though. This time it was a sewer club off Molesworth Street. Knew who he was meeting this time too. He had a name, Kaiser, not just a door in a building somewhere. Kaiser, a big dud with a golden chin, and Spit had to give him a letter, a real piece of paper and say 'Blyss sent me'. Just like Tobin. But he had forgotten Tobin.

He dropped the shuttle at Central and took the substreet to the Old Parliament Memorial. Just a jog from there to the basement where the club was. Easy look for a slick with his wits about him. A flight of steps leading down and a light and a doorway, tight shut, bolted maybe, but he could tell somehow there was an aspect to it, jack, a kind of heat or noise you couldn't feel or hear.

His mind flicked back again to the fat slink's scream and the White Rabbit's cry. A freako feeling, jack, the way that stuff had worked up into him. And the fat slink dressed like that, like a roman emperor, or a Greek. A Greek goddess, was that right? A human sacrifice? The memory of that thrill of fear when her nails ripped through the blond dud's blue-white skin. The brainjoy, had to be. Because part of him wanted to do it all again.

He turned the handle and the door opened, never had a doubt. A passageway inside, a flight of concrete steps. It was all empty but there was real feel heat now, down below, and a sound, a kind of low throbbing. He ran down the stairs, the first flight and the next. There were five, twisting one beneath the other. Down, feeling strong and easy, ASP with touch.

It was a cripples club, he saw it soon as he did the door. A low-ceilinged room with battered tables and old chairs, mattresses against the wall and people missing legs and hands and feet, with twisted backs and lipless mouths. The air was full of smoke, a blend of green and blue, and fudge and stuff he'd never smelled before. There was a big vid on one wall showing film of a car crash in slo-mo, twisting metal and powdered glass.

Kaiser would be sitting in a corner. There, he was there, jack. Well, there were two of them there, at the best table in the place. One was a big dud, brown butcher, wearing a suit with a white shirt and black tie. He had black hair and a beard. Except the beard wasn't right. At the front and to the left there was a bare patch, hole, and through it glint, a yellow flash as he turned his head. It wasn't gold. It was brass maybe. Spit stepped forward, picking his way through the crips towards the table, stepping round the mattresses and the things that lay there. Not looking down. The holes in people and the smoky air were queasy in his guts. But he didn't want to look at that shiny jaw, either. Somehow that was worse.

It wasn't until he got to the table that he got a glim of the second dud. He was hiding almost, squashing himself back into the corner. A geri, maybe, thin, with silver hair, sitting with his arms folded and staring at the back of his wrist.

"Mr Kaiser?" Spit said, standing there.

Kaiser looked up at him. The other one didn't move, though, kept his eyes down so's not to meet Spit's, made sure their eyes didn't meet.

"Who the hell are you?" Kaiser staring, surprised. The flesh round the brass plate was red, curled inwards like a lip.

"I got a message. Blyss sent me."

The look changed then. Angry was it now? Or scared? No, the scare was from the silver-haired dud maybe, who gave a twist in his chair and then sat forward, grabbing at a glass from the table like that was what he was intending to do all along. He drank from it.

"Well, what's the fucking message?" Kaiser said.

Spit gave him the envelope, watched him as he read it.

"So," he said, folding the paper and slipping it into his jacket pocket. "Who are you, then?"

"He's a droppo," said Silver Hair. Which was a pissdick thing to say; and shit, where did it come from except the night in that bar? Tobin night.

"Well," Kaiser said. "Fuck off then."

"Is there an answer?"

"Not that I'd give to a dolly dick like you."

"Go on, droppo. Fuck off!" Silver Hair said.

And then Spit blew his cool. Well shit, that wristic fart, pissing through his mouth. "Listen here, jack, and listen good," he said. "If I'm a droppo you're a fuck geri mushbrain.

Better know I work for the White Rabbit. And you're in it."

Kaiser started to laugh but Silver Hair's eyes sprang like crazy balls. "You little shit!" And he was grabbing after Spit over the table, clutching with a white fist. Spit stepped back and trod on something. There was a yell from down near his left knee, but he didn't wait to look. He was gone, jack, running, pushing and jumping over the bodies. A big shout went up from everyone. A cackle of laughter. Guts in terror twisting. But it was cool, jack. The crips were only creaming over another smash, the screen splattered with blood. He made it to the door and sprinted up the stairs.

10

Be at Peace!
Find Happiness!
Know the Future!

Software of the Sages
Brings You
a Divinely Inspired Emulation of

His Most Holy, Holy Ever Loving
Light of Wisdom
Source of Universal Peace
Sri Mee Kushka Bimba

Officially Approved by the Great Teacher Himself
This Integrated Path to Wisdom Package Offers You

Multi-Media Mandala Module
Fully Configurable Mantra Chanter
Hands-On Natural Random Divination

Seven Genuine Divine Rituals to Choose From!

Runs on any ISI BUBI compliant home station

ONCE ONLY OFFER $745

Fold-in distributed with *Solo Magazine*

Lavendar Tempest with honey blonde hair and a suit of cream synxette, soft and shiny with a short skirt, gold high-heeled shoes. A gold bracelet, too and gold round her throat, gleaming against her white skin. Golden girl, she thought, as she surveyed herself in the mirror, and laughed that she could be so self-satisfied and not care a button.

The elevator slid to a stop on a cushion of air and the doors opened. A small reception suite to one of the Colosseum's big halls. It had dark blue carpet, soft lights and brass fittings. All straight lines and sharp angles, the current style, although she had begun to feel unsure exactly how current it was. Perhaps this part of the Colosseum was becoming just a little passé?

Opposite the elevator were two big wooden doors and a pair of doormen to match; hulking brutes in pale blue uniforms. Lavendar stepped towards them, recognised one of them from a previous event she'd been involved in organising. Michael, was it? He touched his hat, grinned a wide fence of big white teeth.

"Evening, Ms Tempest." He swung the door open.

"Hello, Michael." She gave him a little nod of recognition but then quickly shifted her focus to the way before her and stepped out with her head up, shoulders back, smiling already for the entrance.

Such a fine room, huge space with its hard, polished floor and enormous chandeliers of ice-mass crystal, geometry in glittering chunks. All around, high up on the walls, were rows of glass-like windows, dark behind them where the viewing gallery was. Below these hung a row of huge vids, like banners in a medieval hall. Each one was playing a different motif, constant rows of flashing colour. The Display Team had done well.

Her attention shifted from the surroundings to the people, standing in groups or walking around being seen. In evening dress, of course. Men with shirt fronts white and stiff and black bow ties; the women decked with diamonds, which sparkled like the chandeliers. It was inevitable that any ZIG event would have all the aura of a formal occasion, such distinguished supporters. She spotted media people and entertainment gurus. And the young and fashionable. People like Fiona Duncannen and Saigo Bruce. And Fiona's father Hamish would be here too. Along with Edmond Eliades and even Ronald Chaeffer, perhaps. ZIG was one issue on which the Big Three all agreed. Yes, she could see Hamish over there. He was easy to pick because of the little crowd around him as he crossed the floor. A solid man of medium height with a reddish face and blond hair cropped into a military cut.

"Lavendar, darling! You look absolutely marvellous!" Solveig Robollo, Carl's wife. She was wearing a dress with a black silk sheen and a modest quantity of diamonds, at neck and wrists and hanging from her ears. Lavendar leant forward and gave her a little kiss on the side of her jaw. What was her perfume? Vicious by Gloria Bolton? Solveig was getting daring.

"Wonderful to see such a crowd," Lavendar said. "Doesn't it just show what progress Delwyn's making?"

"Oh, I think ZIG is here to stay, my dear."

"I must say you are looking very well," Lavendar told her. "I do like your hair." It was a severe sort of style, short and layered in softly frosted panels of grey and brunette along the sides.

"This is supposed to be my natural colour." Solveig touched Lavendar gently on the wrist. "Apparently it makes me dignified." She gave a little secret-sharing grin. "Can you imagine that?"

"Always the lady, Solveig."

Solveig laughed. "You're delicious. Why don't we have coffee sometime? In fact, you shall have an appointment. Siobahn?" She beckoned and her secretary stepped forward. Solveig smiled and turned away.

Siobahn was looking her prettiest, blonde in a white dress with a plunging neckline and a short, tight skirt. She took a black schedule connector out of a tiny diamante studded bag, but before she could open it, Lavendar leaned forward and stopped her with a little gesture.

"Call me," she said.

Best not to be condescended to, unless it was absolutely necessary. And coffee with Solveig Robollo, although undoubtedly useful, was hardly a must.

Suddenly, there was a big aah! from the crowd and a sudden burst of applause. A flat disc about a metre and a half across had descended from the roof, and standing or suspended beneath it was a hologram – a banjax player, in a green and purple uniform, limbs set in a half-crouch action pose, black jack in its right hand. The colours of the three dimensional surface were bright, glowing with a bristling kind of aura.

"Ah," Siobahn said. "Isn't he wonderful?"

"Fabulissimo!" A few metres away Solveig was clapping her black gloved hands. "Absolutely fabulous!"

As Lavendar watched, the figure began to move, rising to its feet, one hand on hip. It gave a little bow of its head.

"Hi, there," it said, in a deep voice.

"Hello," said a woman in a white evening dress who was standing to Lavendar's left. The figure turned towards her.

"Good evening, ma'am. So nice to meet you. I trust you're a supporter of Delwyn Tanner."

Everyone was staring, fascinated. Lavendar watched them watching and felt a warm glow of satisfaction. It had been her idea to provide some electronic entertainment for the occasion, and the marketing people at Startech, one of the companies she was attempting to sign up as a client, had been delighted with the opportunity. Now their support of the ZIGs was obvious without being too overt and the gala was already on the way to being a success. Moments like this confirmed her in her career choices, the industry she was working in. How nice it was to achieve such a happy blending of the various elements in her life. Her private interests, her political principles, her social success all seemed to work together so happily with her talent for helping people present themselves to the best possible advantage. A parsimonious elegance, was that the phrase?

◊

Let's go, let's go, let's go, let's GO! Ratman with his search program RFT, R for Roly, F for Froggy, T for Track. It was all written and ready and poked on in there, linked up with the network management system at Southern's Operations Centre. Had a screen now hooked up into that. Hi-rez visual of where the performance problems were. See the roller rolling node to node and generating blasts of stuff and Ratman waiting, hating waiting. Watching for the pattern, watching for where Froggy liked to go, the kinds of systems, where to set the trap. The Froggy Trap a clever, clever program, cunning Ratman. Click the trick in the perfect place and then it would be bang! It would be Ratman and Froggy. Prince Ratman downs the Green Monster. Present for the queen, Queen Cool Eyes. Then she'd see. Then she'd know how Ratman was a prince not a problem, Ratman Hero, Clever Head, doing everything to make it nice for her. Ratman had been to Cool Eyes Country, mean queen scene, and didn't like it. No, no, no. Oh, boy. Respect, lady, that's what you need, respect for the Ratman, know what that means? Ratman lives in cockroach heaven, stays at home and does the stuff, that doesn't mean it's a fuckhead, lady. Has a thought our Ratman, has the pride. It sees!!! It KNOWS!!! You understand??? But don't get shouty. Ratman catches Froggy and the queen will smile again, you bet. Bet you, Charlie, then you'll like it. Bet you, too, the Ratman gets your fuzzy puzzle done. That little NPC number. Ratman already scanned the stuff and sees how it could be, knows it could be, would be. Then you'll know who's mad.

◊

Spit in a wristic bloody outfit for sure, jack. Black suit, white shirt, black bow tie. Felt like a gung tricked out for graduation. SKB. Blyss had hired the gear from a spot on Lambton called Moss and Maunders. Said it was all for authenticity because Spit had to do a real wriggly run. The Colosseum, fourteenth. Conference hall, grand gala for the ZIGs, all the stars would be there. Spit had to slip a dataslice to Frank Biling.

He stood in the main lobby watching the guests arrive. Didn't see no stars, but then he didn't see no chance of getting through the doors himself either. Entrance was by invitation only and the sec cameras were keeping an eye on all the entries, checking each face against a database and warning the butchers on the door, he figged. Shit of a situation, jack, because it meant he couldn't get too close himself to have a look. He thought of calling Blyss up on the cellphone and then decided, no. He was the ASP, jack, do it himself. And there had to be a back door, didn't there? Deliveries, stuff like that. They didn't bring all the shit in over the red carpet.

He took the elevator down to the floor below, a shopping plaza, and wandered round the precinct, looking for a service elevator or a set of stairs. The camera eyes were watching here too but it was public biz. There would be miles of play to look through. Nobody would notice Spit if he was careful. So he tried a few doors, all locked. Peered through the glass into concrete stairwells. Nothing in there but the pissers, eh, jack. But that was it though, wasn't it? Somebody had to take a piss some time. Only had to wait.

And it didn't take too long. After maybe fifteen minutes he spotted a dud in a blue uniform slip out of a florist's, head for the stairs. Spit was after him, timed it right, to perfection, jack. Just reached the door as the dud slipped through it, caught it before it closed. The dud looked a bit freaked but Spit gave the big ASP grin of confidence.

"Hi," he said. Turned and went on up the flight of steps before the dud could answer. Easy, jack. There were cameras here too but...

On the floor above, another door. Through the glass, this time, he could see a kind of service area. Duds dressed like he was, moving about with trays of food and glasses. Got it in one, jack. He waited until someone came close to the door and

then he banged on it. Vague head turn as the dud wondered...
Then he spotted Spit waving. Let him in.

"Not supposed to do this. Where's your card?" the dud said.

"Dropped it, jack. Hey, you know..." Spit moved on past, didn't give the sucky a chance. He was in now. Easy. Grabbed a full tray of drinks and headed out through the doors after the others.

Shit, this was one thing, jack! He had to stop himself from just standing there and staring at the glass chandeliers, the vids hanging from the walls, the holograms around the floor. The place was crammed. Suits and glitter way all over. How the hell to find Biling in a jam like this?

He began to move about with the tray of drinks. Easy to get rid of them, jack. People just grabbed them as he went past. Only problem was he finished up with half a tray of empties. He sidled over to a corner of the room and put the tray down on the floor behind a pot plant. Scooted off away from it as fast as he could.

Then he had the luck, Spit's luck. Just came across Biling standing with a group. Not talking, just standing there like he didn't know what to do with himself. Easier to get the dud's attention out of there, jack. He touched Biling's arm.

"Hi," he said. "Got a message."

Biling looked at him and took it bad. White, he went, like a real freak scare. But he was cool enough to step back a couple of paces so that he and Spit were by themselves. Spit gave him the carry and dataslice.

"Blyss sent me," Spit said.

Biling stuck it in his pocket, carry and all.

"Hey," Spit asked. "You supposed to do the code in there."

"Fuck off." Biling turned his back.

"Hey!" But Spit couldn't cut too much. Not here. And what the hell, jack, anyway. It was only one carry. Blyss had dozens more in a cupboard back at the office.

So he wandered off and looked at a hologram, grabbed a drink from the tray of a passing waiter, wondered how he was going to get out of the place at this stage of the proceedings without being obvious on the pissing cameras. Well, maybe he'd have to hang around a while. This was his last run of the day. He was off duty now anyway.

"Hi," It was a slink, young, skinny, with frizzy black hair. A black dress with a scoop neck that showed the bony bits. A sparkler on a gold chain. A real sparkler, maybe.

"Hi," Spit said.

"My name's Calliope," she said, hold out her hand. "Stupid name, isn't it?"

Her fingers long and cool and bony.

"Seems okay to me, " Spit said.

"Stupid!" Calliope said. "But then I'm stupid so it fits, I suppose." Her eyes were big and brown and blinking slowly, sad looking. A loser, Spit thought, obviously a loser. But if that was a real sparkler she had some clink about her.

"See that woman," Calliope said, pointing to an old slink with short greying hair. "That's Solveig Robollo. She's a bitch."

"I wouldn't know, jack."

"Oh, I would. She's my mother."

"Yer?"

"Yes. And she's also the wife of Carl Robollo. Who is actually my father. They've got blood tests to prove it." She made a dive at a passing waiter and grabbed two champagne flutes. "Here, have some booze."

"Thanks," Spit said. He had two glasses now, one for each hand. He sipped one. It was champagne, he figged. Spit had never tasted it before tonight but he'd seen it on TV. Calliope was staring at him, blinking. Half boozed already, Spit could see.

She looked at him. "Carl's in a tizz tonight. He's not here, don't know why. Mother's still doing her social bit, though."

"Farter and Muddler," Spit said. "FAM."

She laughed. "That's very good. I like that."

Spit grinned at her.

"My muddler's got a special new topic of conversation. Her technopet. You've heard about those?"

"No," Spit said.

"Like animals. Custom built. They run on electricity. Well, you have to plug them in when they're hungry, into a special sort of socket that looks like they're eating a lump of meat in a bowl. That's what Joshua does anyway. Maybe if he was a monkey she'd have to plug him into a banana." She took a long sip of wine.

" Joshua?" Spit asked.

"A snake. A python. Two metres long. Except he's furry, covered in the most beautiful soft hair, brown with cream tips. He loves my mother. Oh, you bet! He crawls all over her." Calliope laughed. "I'm only jealous. I'm only jealous because I don't have one."

A hairy electric snake? Spit might like to see that.

"I'm going to get one, though," Calliope went on. "I'm going to get a baby. One that crawls around after me and says 'Mama'. I can teach it things and plug it into an electric breast attached to me and cuddle it and watch it suck, eh?"

Freako, jack. You bet. But somehow, Spit didn't want to scoot like he might have. Something about this slink that he kind of liked. I mean, not fucking, jack. She was too much of a skeleton for that. Probably fall apart if you touched her. But she had a weirdo sort of scam feel to her. Lively, not like Jank and her sibs. She was a drunken freako, sure, but with a touch of the ASP. Well, maybe.

◊

So ho, ho, ho, and yo, yo, yo. The Froggy Track had done its bit. The Ratman sees his habits now. And knows. He doesn't take to all the gear the same. He likes Q-Pros and Scarabs but he doesn't like DPCs. He likes the Proftek but not the Brownings. Certain kinds of operating system give him the creeps, maybe. Likes the smart stuff, parallel processing, lots of capacity. Likes the entertainment systems, TV and games and interactive movies. Never goes to the down layers, never looks at the old gear underneath. Froggy not been here long then. Or else he grew. From a tadpole maybe, bottom of the pond, but too big for down there now. Has to be a fancy player now.

And so.

And so it's time. It's time for Froggy Trap, the clever little switcher all tricked up now for an ISOS operating system. Ratman saw the spot to put him. A big node. Bottleneck, or would be if it went too slow. A Froggy had to go there some time. Wait and wait and SNAP! And Ratman gottim, pull his innards out and find out how he works. But careful, though. Big boots in a node like that would hurt the traffic. And then customers would not be happy, no, no, no. And Cool Eyes wouldn't like and then Charlie wouldn't like either, growl at Ratman, both go shouty.

Got up, got up and walked the body to the door and back. Checked the Froggy Track screen once more. The roly-poly going. Over to the door and standing there, looking at it. Brown wood panel flat. The little spy hole, eye hole. Tiny world, the corridor out there. Whereas the real world here inside the head was huge, forever open. Ratman knew forever, felt forever. Roly-poly Froggy in his circuits, narrowed down like the corridor. So what would it be like in there among the wires? For that's what Charlie wanted with his NPC, to get from the head world, neural networking, into the hard, right where Froggy was, and meet him face to face. Oh, dumbo, jumbo. Stupid Ratman. Couldn't see a thing like that. For Froggy wasn't real. Or was he?

Breathed, then, leaning the forehead on the door. Breathed again slow. Needed a design, a neural translator for Charlie. Needed the Froggy Trap in the Q-Pro node for Cool Eyes Queen. So who is Ratman's master here? So who's the boss? And Cool Eyes in the neural world could just reach out and touch the brain.

"Oooooooooh!" Noise, a real noise. Who was that? But it was only Ratman, the voice talking like voices do.

◊

"Hello, there." Hot breath in her ear. She turned. Mark Bullington, of all people, leaning over her, smiling, such a big man, dark-haired, in a tux tonight with a red carnation.

"Why, Mark, what a lovely surprise," she said.

"So, image manager, how do I look?" He stood back, struck a pose, casual, rugged. Such an interesting scar he had, a narrow little worm running down from the corner of his mouth towards his lower jaw. It always intrigued her. She had been tempted to suggest he get it fixed but could never quite manage to.

"I'm learning, wouldn't you say?"

"You're doing very well," she told him. "And isn't it working nicely for you? I saw that cover of *Better Day*."

"The story was bullshit." Frowning now, angry suddenly. Sexy when he was angry.

"Of course," she told him. "But it was image true. Banjax is a brutal sport. Half of those readers want to know how tough and unprincipled you are. The other half want to believe you're hard done by."

A few metres away to her left she spotted... Good Lord, it was Frank Biling from Galen. What was he doing here? A lab technician in company like this?

"Anyway," she said, "I bet your fan mail's increased."

"I must confess it has."

Biling was standing alone in the crowd, looking distinctly uncomfortable in a tux, his collar tight, his bald head shiny with perspiration. Behaving oddly? Maybe she ought to keep an eye on him. Introduce herself, perhaps. In a moment or so.

"Our next step is to look a little to the future," she said.

"I can't wait." Smiling that sexy wounded smile. Coming on to her. Well, wouldn't that be interesting then?

"Tomorrow," she told him. "Unless you're going to stand me up again."

"I wouldn't dream of it."

◊

Called up Cool Eyes, yes, oh, yes. She was somewhere with a lot of books.

"Don't you ever stop working?" she asked.

"Ratman n-never sleeps."

"Ratman? Is that what you call yourself?"

"Code name."

"Really?"

Smile, Cool Eyes, smile. But no, no, no. She couldn't and she wouldn't. And Ratman didn't have a joke to make her laugh. Except his own poor self, maybe. Fool of a boy.

"N-need to set the trap. N-n-need a Q-Pro or some such. Want the RMDI4261 n-n-n-node."

"That's high traffic. That's a crux."

"Y-yes."

"Yes. Well, I guess it would have to be, wouldn't it?" Looked serious, oh, so serious. Her thinking eyes. "You'll have to shut it down?"

"M-might. Might crash too."

"We'll lose data. When will this be? No, you don't need to answer that. I know you can't tell me."

"N-n-no."

"Well." Shoulder shrug, her bolder shrug. "I guess we'll just have to wear it. I'll call the centre. Tell them okay."

"G-g-g-good."

"Anything else?"

Everything else. Everything, everything.

"Smile, lady. Smile." The Ratman said.

"Yes," she answered. "You're right." And she did so smile.

◊

"Mr Biling, isn't it? Good evening," she said, offering her hand. "My name's Lavendar Tempest. I've been doing some of the image management work for Galen."

He stared at her for a moment as if he'd never heard of a company by that name. "Oh, hi," he said. His palm was warm and damp, disagreeable, very.

"And how's it all holding?"

"Holding?"

Surely, he must know what she was talking about.

"Your little awkwardness."

"It's holding okay."

"No unpleasant enquiries, I hope?"

"No." He took a gulp from his wine. "Nothing much. Nothing we can't handle."

If only you knew, she thought, how much you have to thank me for. Except that he probably wouldn't thank her. He didn't seem the sort of person who would remember to thank anybody. Unpleasant man. So boorish.

"So what exactly is your connection to the gala?" she asked.

"I'm here, well, I'm looking for a friend of mine."

"Oh, really, maybe I can help. I know a lot of people. I'm a member of the organising committee."

"It's Carl Robollo, actually."

Robollo? Curious, a lab technician socialising with a world expert in electro-neural technology.

"Have you known Carl long?"

"A while. We've worked together a while." He seemed uncomfortable, eyes wandering, anxious. Looking for Carl, perhaps? But then, suddenly, an expression of surprise, fear almost, staring past her.

She turned. No one except a young woman. Who was it? The Robollos' daughter, yes. With a young man.

"Ah, Calliope," she said, attracting the girl's attention.

"Ah, it's you." Calliope seemed half drunk and her companion was an odd looking fellow, scrawny with very shiny, slicked down hair. A pimple or two. Distasteful.

"Hi, jack," he said. To Biling. And Biling didn't answer, just stared.

So? Even more curious. Biling was upset by this pimple face.

"Mr Biling's looking for your father," she said to Calliope.

"He's not here. Gone somewhere urgent. Panic attack."

And that upset Biling even more. He just turned away without a word, strode off on his stumpy legs, pushing his way through the crowd. Lavendar turned back to Calliope.

"Please introduce me to your friend," she said, leaning forward, giving the girl a smile.

"Friend?" Calliope slurped at her glass, turned to the boy. "I don't know. What's your name?"

"Spit," he said.

"Spit? How nice." Lavendar smiled at him, too. "You know Mr Biling?"

He shrugged. "Sure."

"Socially?"

"Business."

"Ah. And who are you with?"

He looked just a little awkward. "Er, David Livid Enterprises."

Suddenly, Calliope was pulling at his arm. "Come on," she said. "I want more booze." Pulling him away, staggering in her shoes, her bony ankles wavering.

"That's such a pretty little dress!" Lavendar called after them.

"Such an angel!" Calliope said over her shoulder.

Lavendar watched them go, wondered quite what had happened, why Biling had rushed away like that and who or what David Livid Enterprises were. None of it was at all significant really, except that she was still suspicious about Myerson and Robollo and Biling's behaviour in the test. And now there was the spotty boy, such a very strange business associate. And what was he doing with the Robollos' silly daughter?

◊

Freako, jack. Fronting Biling again that way with that real touch slink asking the questions. Spit allowed Calliope to pull him along, stood awkward while she grabbed two more glasses from a waiter's tray, accepted one of them. (He had two again now.) What to do?

"I'm pissed, aren't I?" Calliope said. "I'm always pissed, you know that?"

"Maybe you should cut it home," Spit suggested.

"Fuck home! I need food. I want to eat, eat, eat. Come on!" She wobbled off, straight through a hologram of a movie actress, which rippled over her like a luminous freaking skin disease. Beyond it was a long table with plates of food. Calliope reached out and grabbed two handfuls of stuff.

"Behold the news!" she said, holding her arms in the air like a dud in a temple.

Spit looked up too, at the rows of windows round the hall, caught a glimpse up there of a pale, blurred line. Faces, were they? Looking in? Hey, jack. The ords up there, the suckies, all looking down admiring the rich and famous. And I'm down here, jack. Hey!

It made him feel weird. On the one hand, he didn't want to be noticed. On the other, here he was with the real turbs and a high class chick, even if she was pissed out of her head.

"Fuck!" Calliope said, her mouth smeared with white stuff, cheese, and red, peppery stains across her tits. She grabbed another glass of wine and swigged at it. "Oh, shit, I'm pissed." She laughed. "And isn't that a stupid thing to say? What sense does it make? 'Shit, I'm pissed.'"

I should dump her, Spit thought. But maybe not. Maybe there was a real chance here. An angle into something.

"Calliope?" It was a blonde slink in a short white dress. "Are you all right darling?"

"Fuck off!" Calliope said.

"Your mother's worried about you."

"Oh, oh, oh!" Calliope flapped her hands, waving people away. Little blobs of sticky food shit flicked over the blonde's dress and neck.

"Well, damn you!" she said and stomped off back to where she came from.

"That's Siobahn, my mother's secretary" Calliope said. "She plugs Joshua in when mother doesn't have time. Poor Joshua!"

Calliope looked sick, jack, like she might throw up any minute.

"Hey," Spit said, "hey, listen."

"You're my friend, aren't you?" Calliope said. "Here, have some pudding." She reached out, grabbed some glazed fruit from the table, offered it to Spit in a gleaming sticky blob.

"No thanks, jack."

"Why 'ot? Good for you!" She said and threw up over her shoes.

11

**Kill! Kill! Kill! Kill! Kill, kill, kill!
Kill! Kill! Kill! Kill! Kill, kill, kill!
Kill! Kill! Kill! Kill! Kill, kill, kill!
Kill! Kill! Kill! Kill! Kill, kill, kill!**

Paula Flesch of *Death by Sound*

"Is this it?"

"What?" The driver's voice was twisted into a bark by the intercom. He glared over his shoulder.

"Constance Towers."

"185 Willis Street, mate. Right there."

Spit turned on the plastic seat, peered through the back window. Shit, jack, empty pavement in the blue-black light, a drift of litter in an angle of the building. Should've taken the tubestreet, he thought. Except that Calliope was too pissed to walk. Nothing outside except an entrance, big and dark, a drive-under by the look of it. He pointed.

"What say you drop us in there, jack?"

"Forget it, son."

Calliope was slumped in the corner of the cab, eyes closed, white face. Her breath smelled of spew. Spit nudged her.

"Looks like home, jack," he said. "I fig."

"Wha..." She lurched upright, peered out of the wrong window, keeled backwards into Spit's shoulder.

"Youse going to pay and get out?" the driver demanded. "Or you going to sleep in there? Maybe I should start the meter again, eh?"

Spit dropped a twenty coin into the pay slot and yanked at Calliope's arm. "Come on, sister," he said, opening the door.

Outside, standing in the cold. The cab pulled away with a roar and a big belch of fumes and they were left like naked, jack. Nothing but the other cars on the street, their lights yellow, drifting past. A damp wind fingering their faces. Could be anything out here. Could be street jackers. Could be Tobin. Now what?

But Calliope was heading up the ramp into the drive-under. There was a stagger in her walk but she knew where she was at. Spit followed her into the big, echoing cave. It was pitch black round the angle. Silence. Then a shift and a movement and suddenly the place was full of light and there was a siren blaring and a thing like a heap of rags was hobbling away on two thin legs.

Spit yelled but the siren drowned him out. The noise went on. A pair of elevator doors slid open. Calliope, with her hands over her ears, staggered inside. Spit, too, made it and the doors closed and the sound stopped.

"Shit!" Spit said.

Calliope was leaning against the steel side of the elevator panting. "Hate it, hate it, hate it."

A bland butcher male voice through a speaker somewhere. "Miss Robollo, is that you? Can you confirm please?"

"It's me! Fuck!" Calliope yelled.

"And your companion?"

"Friend of mine." A mutter this time.

"Name please."

Silence. Spit stared at the honeycomb roof. Scam, he thought.

"Cartington," he said. "Andrew Cartington." As good a fuckin name as any, jack. A real class name.

The lift started to move, a little lurch and a smooth acceleration, up. The floor indicator flickered through tens, twenties, thirties. Slowed and stopped. Floor forty-one. Calliope levered herself upright and stood there swaying. The doors stayed shut.

"Hate it, hate it, hate it," she yelled and thumped the wall with her fist.

"Miss Robollo, can you confirm you wish Mr Cartington to enter the apartment?" the voice said.

"Are you saying I'm pissed, Hamburger?"

"No, ma'am."

"Open the fucking doors before I throw up in here!"

The doors opened. A little lobby with soft lights and plush carpet, an art vid showing, picture of a night sky with a big swirl of stars like milk. Calliope wobbled to the door and slammed her hand against the grey lockplate, blundered through when it opened, down the hallway yelling, "I'm home, everybody! I'm home!"

Spit followed, shut the door behind him like a class act and walked along between a double row of vids that lined the walls. They were old paintings, all of them, stuff with proper touch like there was clink here, jack, you could smell it. Couple of doors half open on the right but there were no lights on so it was hard to see. Weird, the feeling of a joint like this. Another kind of place. Made you wonder why they did things, how their minds worked. Having the stuff like these turbs did.

Calliope was in the kitchen gulping straight from a plastic bottle of orange juice.

"Drink?" she said. "Wine? A whisky?"

"Shit, jack, no. A coffee, maybe."

"Be my guest!" A wide sweep of her arm like she was offering it all, and then she sat down on a stool at a kind of bar, pulled a face, shook her head.

"Nobody home?" Spit asked, looking around for a kettle or a coffee maker.

"Only us. And Joshua. He's here somewhere. Fucking snake! She cares more about that fucking snake than she does about anybody. Is that right? You tell me, is that right?"

There was nothing among the electronic stuff round the walls and the kitchen bench that looked like it could make a cup of coffee so Spit gave up, settled instead for a bottle of soda from the refrigerator.

"No, jack," he said, "it's not right."

"Fuck 'em all! Shiiiiit!" Calliope yelled it, doubling herself over so that dregs from the juice bottle in her hand dribbled over the red tiled floor.

"Where are they?" Spit asked.

"Still at the Gala, I expect. That stupid, fucking ZIG do. Or wherever. I hate 'em, you know that?"

"What? ZIGs?"

"Hate 'em!"

"Don't know much about it, jack."

"That's cos you've got brains. Anybody with brains stays clear of it."

"Maybe it's cool. They say it's cool, but I dunno."

"Cool?" Calliope gave a freako sort of laugh. "It's vicious, jack, and you don't know the half of it. Boy, I could tell you."

"Like what?"

"Oh, boy." Calliope shook her head like there was so much she didn't know where to start.

"Like what?" Spit repeated.

"Stuff they do. The dirty stuff, the dealing. I mean, you know, they tell you all about democracy and it's just bullshit. They stitch things up in corners all over."

"Free market, isn't it, jack?"

"Competition. You tell me, if competition's so good, then why are they always trying to get the drop on each other, eh?"

"All's fair, jack." Spit couldn't figure what she was on about. Political freako. Was she a Jesser maybe? Couldn't be with the clink that was round here.

"Everything just becomes like sport, that's all. Like a fucking banjax game. Absolute sickos, that's what they are."

Maybe she was right. Spit had never thought about it before. All those people, like they were all doing their stuff. It gave him a weirdo feeling to think how different their lives were and made him think again about the Queen of Heaven and the White Rabbit, red nails cutting into pale flesh, the shiver of it. Shit, jack, why'd he think of that?

"That butcher there tonight," he said. "Biling. The baldy

who was talking to the slink with the gold shoes."

"What about him?"

" What's he do?"

"Don't know. Used to work with my father when he had his own company. Used to be a software designer. Lost it now, though, I think. Something he did. Dad found him a job at the hospital."

And Biling had a real scare about Blyss. There was something going on, jack, he knew it. ASP with his feelers out, sensing stuff.

"Hate it," Calliope was muttering, "hate it." And then, suddenly, she was yelling and off her stool, across the room, kicking at something on the floor, an arm-thick writhing thing that looped and twisted, cream brown knots, and hissing plaintive gasps and it was gone, out through the door with a frantic flap of its fluffy pointed tail.

"Fucking snake!" Calliope yelled after it. "Why can't you stay and fight?" And she burst into tears, stood there sobbing with her pale arms like sticks, her long bony hands over her face. Spit went and stood near her, not knowing quite what to do and she put her arms round him, hugged him tight, her head buried in his shoulder.

"Hey," Spit said. "Hey, it's okay."

"Are you my friend?'

"Sure, jack, yes. Abso-fuckin-lutely. AFL."

"Just don't call me a slink, that's all."

"Sure, jack. Sure."

"I don't care who else you call that, but not me, okay?"

"No problem," Spit told her.

"And you're going to keep on liking me?"

"I have to, jack. Don't I?" And weird, oh, so weird, he had tears in his own eyes, jack.

◊

Ratman, easy. Headset on. A little throb as he fixed the call signal out into the network. Ratman calling. Worktime done now, time for fun now. Lying on the bed, the Rat's Nest, thinking of Froggy and Charlie Cato and Queen Cool Eyes. Angel Cool Eyes. Made her smile again, the clever Ratman, felt the flow of things, the know of things. How Cool Eyes smiled. So make her happy, Ratman. Catch the roller. Bring it home to her on a plate and then she'll... What will she do? The Ratman doesn't know.

– Hello, there.
– Who's that?
– Ratman, is that you? It's Cabber here.
– Hey, Cabber, man. How ya goin?

Cabber showed him a video of the sun going down over the sea, a slow pan, left to right.

– Cool, baby. Takin' a break. We're at day's end here on the eastern seaboard. Where're you at?
– Ratman doesn't count, Cabber. Some time.
– What you workin' on?
– NPC. Neural translator.
– You in cuckoo-land, Ratman?
– Got an idea. Got a goer. Got the chips and got the chassis.
– What kind of chips?
– Cortechs FTPs. 6070s. Had 'em here in my store kit all the time.
– You're crazy, man. Let me know, though.
– Got a roller here too, Cabber, a froggy. Runs in ISOS.
– Hey man, take care with that. Waldo had one of those. Tried to copy it and it trashed three systems on him. Bad PR.
– Nasty, nasty. Customer bustimer.
– Something like that.
– Cool Eyes wouldn't smile.
– Who's Cool Eyes?
– Customer, Cabber. Real sexy piece, a blonde.
– A good looking chick? You lucky, man.
– She freaks the Ratman.
– You in love?
– What's love, Cabber?

– You know love, Ratman. Boy meets girl. Boy fucks girl. Blow your mind like a real neural jag.
– Girls on the nightfix.
– They're not girls. They're addicts, man. Like you and me. I mean body fucks. Not mind fucks.
– Ratman doesn't do that. Cool Eyes neither. Bad for you.
– Who says?
– You ever do that, Cabber?
– What?
– Body fuck.
But Cabber gone. Run away. Faded. Ratman waiting, calling. Anybody out there?
– Don't listen to that creep, Ratman.
Who that? Nobody. Nobody there. The genflak coming in all over in coloured streaks of flow. Just watch the pretties, Ratman. Nothing to do but watch the pretties, ditties, cities. All the feel-good flow. The glow. The mind smoothed out, the wrinkles gone.
– Hey, Ratman.
Ratman doesn't care.
– This is Wong Fa World. We love you, Ratman.
Doesn't care and doesn't stare. The mind rolls over, sleepless Ratman filled with the mind sensations, flow gone out into the bright night light and Ratman starts to dream of home, not its own home, never had a home to remember, but a place with a quiet, clean room, a big soft chair, a cup of hot milk and a fire in the grate, the light dark fire that flickered on the warm walls.

◊

Lying on her back in the dark, body floating, yes, a soft relax. Lavendar could have gone to sleep, of course, but she was excited and enjoying it. She had made useful contacts in the course of the evening, had had a conversation with Fiona Duncannen who actually remembered who she was. A nice piece of progress, something like that, really an important piece. Like a seed that had already sprouted on those videos at school, growing quickly because it was speeded up by technology. And it was possible to speed things up. It was possible to make the good things come to you more quickly if you wanted them. She let her mind drift back to the early days, to the time before she first enrolled at university, when she had known nobody and had been nothing but a.... No, it didn't do to go back too far. Didn't need to look into that darkness if she didn't want to. And she didn't want to. Not ever again. And no need even to be afraid of it now, not now, after so much progress and her new family developing so well.

A heavy, gentle peace had settled on her limbs. She could feel sleep pulling at her mind, although her thoughts were still bright and active. It was strange, how it happened, losing consciousness. She never remembered her dreams but there were times, like now, when she could feel the images of somewhere lurking on the edges of her mind like ghosts. No, not ghosts, unless they were the spirits of the future. Faces, bodies moving, nobody she knew and all jumbled up and overlaid. And bits of scenes. Peaceful, her body was so heavy, so comfortable. The tensions of the day flowed out of her like dirty water, leaving her clean and whole and new, and she felt herself sinking, dwindling until suddenly she saw, in an instant, the whole scene, herself and Cynthia and Mummy and Daddy standing on a hillside, wind so free in their hair. And Cynthia laughing, and she was laughing herself to feel how absolutely wonderful her whole life was. And never thought for a moment of an old-looking woman dressed in second-hand clothes from Big Parade.

12

Deficit Report Slams Council

Once again the harsh facts of economic reality have demonstrated the fundamental weakness in the City's infrastructure. The specially commissioned financial report into Combined Council's second quarter budget deficit of $27.4m was released today amid protests from the Mayor's Office and plaudits from corporation watchdogs. Independent consultant Charles Devour concluded that although there were 'no manifest irregularities' in the production of the Council's consolidated financial statements, the deficit was evidence of 'possible inefficiencies' and demonstrated the need for 'further stringencies'. Mayor Layden Baird immediately issued a statement that Devour was 'out of line in coming up with value judgements'. 'This turkey's supposed to be an independent auditor', he said. Corporate chop-person and Eliades think-tanker Carol Carlion said the report 'once again demonstrated that only exposure to market forces and genuine competition can generate the efficiency and energy to run a city like this in today's economic climate'.

Kim Tokia, special correspondent
Full Financials

Spit had a new suit, slick, jack, a real smooth touch in royal blue with a yellow handkerchief in the top pocket and a tie to match. He had a strut to his walk like the city was good. Only his second day on the job and he owned his walk, jack, knew his air was his and not like some welfare wrister told him when to breathe and when to scratch himself. And even now in the mid-morning rain still swirling round the towers like a hail of bullets, wind blowing, even now he could still picture the look on the Farter's face when he took off for the day and the Muddler smiling, proud and scared, too scared to be proud, jack, full of geri-yellow freeze. They couldn't believe it. Made him feel like the ASP of ASPs.

The current run was easy biz. Across the tubestreet, keep out of the rain, over to the Willis Complex, North East Tower. He had a dud to see called Marmaduke, a wristic label, that Blyss said was a special customer. Street was humming on a day like this, like the wind was stirring up the game and everybody blowing with it, walking like they had to; slinks in fashion rags and the suiters, all got jag and tack. The whole place smelt of clink like you could taste it in the air. It was the way, jack. Downtown where the money was and not the pisshole dried up parks, the Naenae Estates, with the geris picking their noses and the walls wet because the roof leaked or the crep upstairs was pissing on the floor again.

Marmaduke was residential. Solid piece of clink to own a place in the Complex. Spit pushed the button, waited while the cameras looked him over, gave his name when the system asked him, used to this by now.

It reminded him of the Robollo place and Calliope the freako sister. She had got out of it nearly total, last night, on more than piss for sure, some other tab, jack. It had been a weirdo scene, what with Calliope peeving and jazzing all over and then her mother and that Siobahn slink coming home with a security guard. None too happy to find Spit there. The guard had butchered him out down the hallway, a shriek from the bedroom where Siobahn was doing stuff to Calliope.

"Come in," a voice from the system speaker said.

The door clicked. He pushed it open, found himself in a square hallway, four doors. They were all shut except the one to the left.

"Come on in."

A kind of office, not so big, with a desk and leather chairs and shelves of books from floor to ceiling. One wall was a window looking out into the rain, the air like swirling grey curtains.

"Comforting, isn't it?" The dud behind the desk was small. He had black hair and a bushy black moustache with a touch of grey like he'd sneezed on it. He sat looking at Spit with his head on one side.

"I'm looking for a Marmaduke," Spit said.

"Yes, of course." The dud smiled, at least he might have been smiling. It was hard to tell because half his mouth was hidden under the whiskers.

"I guess that's you, jack. You got your code?" Spit moved over to the desk and handed over the carry. Marmaduke made an even bigger thing with his face so his mouth looked like a hole. He took the carry in one hand. His fingernails were shiny, Spit noticed. Like he wore nail varnish or else he buffed them up on his lapels he was so pleased with himself all the time.

"Are you party to this affair?" Marmaduke asked.

"Sure," Spit said, wondering what the dud meant.

"Then you'll know how dangerous it is to carry this material. If it were known what's known here, then the whole city would be out to get us." He laughed. "But then, in a sense, that's only fair, given that we're out to get the city, eh?" He gave a quick pull and the dataslice came out of the carry. Marmaduke leaned over to his right and put it in a drawer of the desk.

"Yes," Spit said. "It's a tough game, jack." Wondering how to change the subject. The idea of being got by the whole city was low-level touch in Spit's view, not something to think about.

"I have a reply," Marmaduke said. He was holding out an envelope made of cream coloured paper, thick paper, roughish on Spit's fingertips. The edge of the flap had little bites out of it in a fancy pattern.

"Tell Mr Blyss I wish him well and that I have some small faith in his ability to create the opportunities," Marmaduke went on.

"Sure."

"I'm concerned about the Petone incident, of course. I wouldn't want the Mole to become a nuisance."

"Sure, jack." Not liking this talk much, either. He didn't need to be reminded about the Mole, or about eyes in boxes and Tobin's dispensable associate.

He stuffed the envelope in the inside pocket of his jacket, turned to leave.

"Chaos is Freedom," Marmaduke called after him.

◊

"Let's try and get focused here," Lavendar said. "What, precisely, are we trying to achieve? Something softer? Something more kindly?"

"I wouldn't go that far." Mark Bullington looked almost disgusted at the thought.

"Do you need to do anything? I mean, the old image has served you so well, hasn't it? Roughest, toughest kid on the block?"

"Twice voted dirtiest player in the Senior League, yer, sure. It's just that, well, I'm thirty-four, Lavendar. In two or three years, I'll retire. Call it mid-life crisis, if you like, but I don't want to spend the rest of my days as an ex-heavy. I mean, what do I do, become a TV commentator? Open a bar?"

"The Bull turned out to grass. I see what you mean." She thought for a moment, looked at his face in the vid in front of her. A handsome face, dark hair, dark eyes, a full-lipped mouth with that most intriguing scar. He had an air about him, a curious combination of refinement and brutality. Beneath the macho surface, there seemed to lurk a contrary spirit, not sensitive exactly but complex, powerful feelings at war with one another. She could see why he had acquired all those female fans. And what would it be like, she wondered, if she allowed herself to… Silly. She was not even sure what she meant. Although, of course she was sure. Of course she was.

"I think," she said, "we need to take this gradually. Reveal things a little at a time. What say the Bull has a secret human side, heart of gold, something he's kept hidden for years?"

"You mean charities?"

"I was thinking of something more personal. A child, perhaps, a poor unfortunate that you've taken a special interest in."

"They'll just think it's some bastard I've fathered."

"That's okay. They'll feel all the more guilty when they realise how they've misjudged you."

"Where do we find this kid?"

"You have two choices there. We can look for a real one. Or we can invent something. I know some really good people in the personal development profile business."

He thought about it. Little frown lines between his eyes, lips pressed into a straight line. Perhaps he didn't like children.

"Is there anything philanthropic you're involved with?" she asked.

"I've got some shares in famine relief. My broker says Aid to Africa is about to declare a twenty-two percent after-tax profit for its half year."

Not exactly a deep humanitarian impulse there, she thought. Well, perhaps this was all the wrong tack.

"How about you get engaged?"

"Who to?" He seemed genuinely surprised at the suggestion.

"Or perhaps you could enrol at university."

"Huh." An odd little grunt. Maybe she'd touched a chord now.

"Has anything like that ever interested you?" she asked.

"I..." He looked sheepish, shame-faced.

"When you were a child, for instance. An academic subject you really liked?"

"Nagh!"

"Really?"

"Well, I did have this thing about Ancient Greece for a while," he said.

"Perfect!"

"Nagh," he said. "That's ridiculous."

"Think about it," she said. "And think about the other things we've talked about. None of it needs to be a major commitment. Just enough so that we can start to create some interesting stories, alternatives to your current image."

"Okay." He was preoccupied, she could see, intrigued by something. So she had really touched a chord. Ancient Greece? Perhaps he could learn the language. Now wouldn't that be wonderful?

"Let's talk again in a day or two."

"Sure," he said, looking at her, smiling, turning on the charm again. "Why don't we do it over dinner?"

"Why not?" Smiling herself, then. Testing him, just to see. And he responded, pleased, interested. And needing, immediately, to take control back just a little.

"I'll call you," he said. "Ciao." And faded.

Fascinating, she thought. And wouldn't it be nice to be out on the arm of one of the city's sporting heroes? And afterwards, who knew? Although, of course, there was always Curtis Caid to think of. Not good to have things get too complicated.

A quick log-in to her stockbroker now before she forgot. Aid to Africa shares hadn't moved much for the last month. She entered her PIN number and bought five thousand dollars worth, just a little flutter. Then she checked the office system to see if any messages had come in since she had been talking to Mark.

There was one. Dougall Myerson. Pale face, drawn, looking very serious.

"Lavendar," he said. "I think it only fair to warn you. There's a news item you should look at. Channel 17." That was all.

She sat for a moment. A terrible feeling of misgiving. A shiver, she was sweating. An awful, awful feeling, as if her suspicions had all come true. And yet... She logged into the TV link, calling up the newsbases. Channel 17. Crime news, a quicktext link-in. Why crime? She watched as the numbered headlines began to roll, staring at them. How was she supposed to know which?

Woman Ate Baby, Court Told
Eighty Million! Con-man of the Year!
Happy Valley Slasher Strikes Again
Lab-Man Gutted Near Monument
Geli Glissence Gets Fifty Years!

More?

Which? The Slasher? No. The Lab-Man, it had to be. She clicked the item and there it was. The face, stern like a mugshot, bald head, drooping black moustache and small, hard eyes. And a voice. "...Frank Biling of Austin Street, Laboratory Technician, last seen in the region of Morton's Videodrome. Biling's body was found this morning in an alley off Hill Street. In this ghastly and blood-thirsty slaying, it was hanging from a metal gate and had been disembowelled..."

A shot, a horror shot of the alley, dark with slants of pale light, gate, a metal grill at the end, and a shape there, hoisted up on it. She stared, she couldn't help staring, as the camera moved in and nothing to see with the voice droning on. Biling's head, a pale shape gleaming, slanted to the left, the slump of his body there. And something strange, a kind of glistening tangle dangling from his waist.

She turned away.

"...spokesperson from the PNPC denies any evidence that it was ring related despite rumours that Biling had connections with several ringland associates. A double life for this seemingly mild-mannered medico? We'll keep you posted." And the voice switched suddenly to an ad for electronic soap, the Wash without Water. Lavendar reached forward and punched the off switch.

Feeling cold. Her fingers and toes were damp and chilly, her stomach churning. She was going to throw up, she knew she was going to throw up but then, no, half-way out of her seat she thought she wouldn't, sat down again, lay back with her head, dizzy on the rest and the room turning as the waves of nausea swept through her. Awful, awful, she thought.

To have such a thing happen. They had done this. They had ruined her.

◊

Cool Eyes called.

"So," she said. "How's it going?"

And snowing and blowing.

"T-t-trap set."

"But not sprung."

"N-no."

"Have you seen the latest problem reports?"

"N-n-no."

"More corruptions. We've had a Gloria Bolton ad on prime time television where the models had no teeth. We've had an obscene e-mail broadcast go out to the entire Combined Council. We've had a wildlife programme which describes the cockroach as an endangered species. You'd appreciate that one."

Not smiling now, no, no. Was Cool Eyes mad? Was she mad at Ratman? Wasn't fair to stare and glare.

"Almost like our roller friend has a taste for schoolboy jokes. An adolescent sense of humour."

"Y-y-y-y…"

"You have any news at all for me?"

"He's g-getting b-bigger."

"Bigger?"

"More space, more c-c-code, maybe."

"More transactions generated?"

"Ratman th-thinks so."

"Do you have any good news?"

"Maybe if he's m-making himself bigger means there isn't a c-c-c-copy."

"You mean if we can destroy this one, we'll have got rid of it altogether?"

"Y-yes."

"If we catch it." Cool Eyes unbelieving. Didn't trust

Ratman. Didn't like Ratman. No, not nice.

"Ratman working, tries its b-b-b-best. You know?"

"What?"

Didn't Cool Eyes hear him? Then, she heard. "Sure," she said. Her eyes closed for a second. Smile? Not quite. "We're both under pressure here and, you're right, we certainly need to keep perspective. Look, far as I can see, you're doing your job. Okay?"

"O-o-o-o…"

"It would probably do us both good to have a break and come back to it with fresh minds."

"Th-th-th-th…"

"Why don't you let me buy you lunch?"

Lunch? Punch. Another hairy, scary, out there. Whoa, Ratman.

"Okay?" she asked.

"Wh-wh-where?"

◊

Blyss was out on the biz when he got back so he sat down on the sofa and made himself easy. Watch some TV, jack. Except TV reminded him of the geries and the empty wall vid made him think of the Queen of Heaven. And the Queen of Heaven was the White Rabbit and *that* made him think of the mad geri in the cripple club and the Kaiser, a ruthless bloody butcher if ever there was. So, he wondered maybe if Blyss had left him a message on the cellphone and turned it on.

There was a message for him all right but it wasn't from Blyss. That freako sister, Calliope instead. Hey, how had she got his number, jack? Must have dropped it to her round at her place. Blyss mightn't like it, office info flashed about like that.

Calliope stared at him from the screen. She looked okay, jack. Had her hair done. Tired maybe but who wouldn't be after all the piss'n stuff she'd thrown down her mouth last night.

"Hi, Spit," she said. "Thanks for everything. You know, you're a nice guy. Like, call me if you want. And if you don't that's okay too. See you."

Nice guy? Spit felt a nudge of something, kind of... Didn't know. He didn't know either if he wanted to get alongside such a mad bitch as Calliope. She had clink, though. She had touch, too, in a weirdo sort of way. He got her number out of the message, thought about it for all of two seconds, jack, and called her back on the main phone, vision off.

The Siobahn slink answered, crisp and fresh in a white silk blouse, her long blonde hair draped around her shoulders.

"Good morning, can I help you?"

"Yes, Miss Robollo, please. Calliope."

"May I say who's calling?"

"I'm a friend of hers."

"I'm afraid we have a policy here. We don't take calls from people we can't see."

"I don't have a vid phone here," Spit said.

"Name please." Siobahn was looking like she swallowed her tooth brush, sour faced.

"This is Miss Robollo's hairdresser, I..."

The vid went blank, cut him off. Fuck that, jack. Spit dialled straight back but Siobahn had already flicked the switches. The screen came up with a bunch of yellow flowers in a vase and an answervoice said, "Robollo residence. How may I help you?"

"Good morning, this is Miss Robollo's..." The flowers slammed open to a bald-headed butcher, bloodshot eyes and an ear like big wart. A simulation, Spit figged, triggered by his voice print.

"Listen, cocksucker," it said. "Just piss off."

"Hey, wait on, jack. I..."

"Piss off! And if you don't, I'm going to come round to that shithole little office block you work in and I'm going to shove that fancy data carry right up your arse and pull it out your little shit-filled gob, you understand me?"

Blank screen and staring at it. Fuck, jack, hey! This was

freako. They knew, jack. How did those Robollo turbs find out who he was and where and why? Something happened way too fast, jack. Spit didn't like it. SLS, jack. Stank Like Shit.

◊

Job to do, she had a job to do. And it was a big one. Mess. Such a huge mess, she just knew it. And her sense of betrayal, anger at the way they'd treated her. Biling had betrayed her and Galen too. Because whatever this was, it almost certainly meant... No, she didn't know what it meant. Biling and the failed ENAS test, the doctored security record, a ringland connection. Ringland? Goodness, what if Biling had done it to Derek Mountain deliberately, some contract. And Isis was now implicated in the cover up. How could she keep a lid on that? But she had to do something, didn't she? Couldn't just sit there.

What would Cynthia do in this situation? Silly. Cynthia would never be in this situation, out there on her farm. But still, there were crises on farms, weren't there? Dangers? Horrible dangers sometimes. Cynthia would stay calm. She would be scared but she'd stay calm. She'd take control in a practical way.

– Nothing's that bad, she might say. Nothing's that bad that you can't overcome it with patience and care. And determination. Let your intuition guide you. Goodness, you're not going to let this wreck your whole career, are you?

– No, of course not.
– Begin then.
– Where? The test?
– No. The gala.
– Why the gala?
– Because... Just because. He shouldn't have been there, should he? Not somebody like that. And he behaved oddly. With that spotty boy. And Robollo's daughter. Goodness me!
– The sec record.
– Yes. As a member of the organising committee you can

easily get hold of the security tapes. Tell them it's for trend analysis purposes.

Yes. She was calm now. Knew what to do. Called up the Colosseum and gave her security clearance, asked to get the security tapes down loaded. Then she called Myerson.

He looked tired but she didn't care. Fighting for herself now.

"Lavendar," he said, "this is most unfortunate."

"How do you want to deal with this? Do you want me to act for you?"

"We plan to distance ourselves, one hundred percent. Take whatever actions you think fit."

"I need all the information you have."

"There isn't any. Nothing."

"I'd like copies of Frank's diary and phone records, anything like that."

"I'll talk to our security people."

"What do the police say?"

"No leads."

"Was he responsible for what happened to Derek Mountain?"

"Maybe, who knows?"

"I suppose you have other people apart from Isis working on this."

"Certainly, but that won't affect you. Our strategy at this stage is maximum confusion."

"I'm on my own?"

"That's probably the best way to look at it. For now."

◊

"Ah, yes, indeed. Indeed and indeed." Blyss in the doorway, grinning his grin with the two almost peeping teeth. He was wearing a grey three piece suit and a wristic blue tie. The toes of his polished shoes had little stars in them. "Any messages while I've been away?"

Something in his voice Spit couldn't get. Blyss knew, he figged. Blyss knew about Calliope. Better spill, he thought.

"Yer. I got a call."

"A young person of the female persuasion?"

"Yer. I... She got the number somehow, jack."

"I expect you gave it to her last night..."

"Me, jack?"

"...in the heat of passion, hmmm. And beautifully done it was, my boy. Miss Robollo is a very fine connection for you. A charming young lady with an array of glorious talents. You'll see."

Connection? Spit decided he was never going to fig this freako.

"They scanned me, jack. They know about the biz."

"What biz?"

"The data carry. Back and forth."

"Of course they do. They're not stupid."

"I didn't tell her nothing, jack. She was too pissed. I reck she was lucky to remember her own fuckin' name, let alone the phone number."

"Well, she did remember and they tracked us through it. A lovely situation, really. Perfect. They know who we are. They suspect there's a plan afoot but they don't know what."

"Plan, jack? It was pure luck I nexted her." Wasn't it? For a moment, Spit wondered if Blyss hadn't rigged the whole thing.

"Luck is the best kind of planning."

"So what's with this connection, jack? What's it for?"

"Well." Blyss was thinking, staring at the wall. Then, he seemed to decide. "Before we answer that, you need to understand things a little better."

"Understand, jack?"

"There's someone I think you ought to meet. The next stage in your training, so to speak."

◊

Place all angles, shiny, lots of light. Like summer. Ratman didn't like it, all eyes looking. Turned its head and saw itself, the hair and beard, reflected in the shiny window. Cool Eyes picked a table, Ratman sat. Back to a wall like marble with a kind of creeper, dark green leaves and yellow flowers. Weird the flowers. Hadn't seen a flower since…. Forgotten. And rotten.

Cool Eyes talking. "I figure it can't be good for you locked away working like that. A little variety must help."

"P-plenty of variety." Work, work, work. More, more, more, Charlie. Don't stop, please.

"But a bit short on physical reality, I would have thought. Only ever dealing with the world through vid screens and visors."

"S-s-sokay." Eyes on the table, Ratman. White swirlies in the yellow surface, smooth and clean.

"Too much for me. After ten hours or so, I start to go stir-crazy. And I hate dealing with people that way. At arm's length. You never get to know them. And you can't work effectively with people you don't know."

Somebody standing by the table. Baggy shorts, and pink sneakers. No socks.

"You folks like something to drink maybe?" Waiter. Blond, a T shirt, banjax club badge splat across the chest. And grinning, putting menus on the table. Hurt the Ratman's eyes to look.

"Tonic," the Queen said. "With lemon. How about you?" Asking him and tasking him. But this was easy.

"C-c-c-coke."

"Certainly, sir." The waiterman, smiling, teeth were scary white. He went away.

"So, you said our virus was getting bigger," Cool Eyes said.

"Y-yes."

"Which means the PR problems get worse. Well, that's life, I guess. How long's it been there?"

"D-d-don't know. Maybe it's been g-g-growing for a while. Maybe it started as a teeny-tiny. N-n-never did nothing. Good little boy."

"Any thoughts on where it comes from?"

"D-don't know, maybe. Movies, TV systems. Games

network maybe. S-something with a r-random element." Watching the table, swirly patterns, twirly patterns.

"You mean this thing just happened?"

"M-m-m-m-m..." But yes, and yes, yes, YES. The Ratman see it now, it could be.

"That's crazy," she said. "That means... well, it means... I don't know what it means."

Means it's ALIVE, lady. Couldn't be, though, could it? Cool Eyes right.

"The thing I'd really like to know, though, is what's it doing? Is it behaving randomly or is there a purpose behind it?"

"W-w-which would you like?"

Laugh. She laughed. The Ratman made her. How?

"Well, that's a good question. I guess I don't really care as long as we can keep it under control. Which we probably can't. I fielded another problem before I left the office just now. Galen Laboratories say a surge of input from one of our local networks interfered with a test they were doing and put someone in hospital."

"H-h-how?"

"Apparently their test equipment's hooked up directly to their patient's database. Mad arrangement, if you ask me, but..."

"H-h-hard for Froggy." Even if Froggy was alive.

"You'd think so. Maybe they're just trying it on. It could be an embarrassing case for them."

Waiterman came with the drinks. Set them down. Ratman took the coke, looked up. Cool Eyes watching him with eyes that opened up his whole inside.

"Here's to success," she said, raising her glass.

"Suc-suc-success. And Ratman give you Froggy."

"I sincerely hope so." Laugh again. Oh, boy. The Ratman's heart was pumping, thumping. Head was beating like a drum. Her eyes like nails had fixed him to the wall.

◊

A room back of the office, out through a door down a corridor. Blyss palmed a lock and ushered Spit through. A sudden blast of warm air. Little room with hangings on the walls like fancy carpets and the same all across the floor. There was a door on the far side and, in the corner, a pile of cushions and a wristic little table with a tall brass pot or jug on it. A sultan's palace, cell. A slap of Eastern touch. But a familiar feel to it, though. Like he'd been here before, jack, but couldn't have.

"This is it, for the moment," Blyss said, grinning. "I'll have to leave you here but please, pray, sit, be thankful."

"What's the deal, jack?"

But Blyss was going, moving back through the door, and before Spit could give a squawk he was out. The wood shut, lock clicked home. And that was it, jack. Shafted.

Spit opened the other door and found no more than he expected. A little bathroom and kitchen sort of thing. A bedroom with a bed all made. It looked good. Neat with the wristic touch of all that Eastern shit, but there was no way out.

He went back to the room with all the carpets on the walls and sat down on the cushions. Cross-legged, jack. He'd seen it in the movies.

The inner mysteries? Right, jack. SKB.

13

These are the Readers We Don't Want

If you answer yes to more than three of the following questions, SAVE YOUR MONEY. We don't want your nose in our magazine.
- Are you over fifty?
- Are you on welfare?
- Are you married?
- Would you like to be married?
- Do you ever go driving in the country?
- Do you shop at Big Parade?
- Do you like children?
- Do you listen to the Bland Brothers?
- Would you like to live anywhere but Solo City?
- Did you vote for Layden Baird?

Solo Magazine

She took Biling's image from the tape of the test, together with one of herself and locked a search onto them. She then let this run through the data from the six security cameras at the ZIG gala. The two target spots began to dance over the six windows in her vid wall. Ten times normal speed. They came together finally on camera five: 8.37 p.m. She slowed it, brought in the zoom.

There! Biling and herself talking and Calliope coming up to them, with the spotty one. She took the speed back to normal, focused on the young man. He was the clue, wasn't he? Such an odd person to be there. Shiny hair so full of grease. She gave a little shudder at the thought. Then she locked the search facility onto him and wound the system back, trying to find a moment when... Yes! There he was glancing up at camera four.

– What do you think of him, Cynthia?
– Up to no good.
– Oh, yes, I'm sure you're right.
– A kind of animal cunning.
– Oh, yes, I think so.
– Get him traced?
– Oh, yes.
– Let's just look a little more first.

She scanned back all the way through the gala records, saw how Spotty Face came in through the waiters' entrance, tracked him as he wandered about, saw how he'd had an initial brief conversation with Biling and how he'd then latched onto Calliope and finally left with her. Did something change hands in that first encounter? It was hard to tell, the two of them partly obscured by the crowd. But intensity in Biling's manner, agitation.

Say Spotty gave him something. And later on the same night Biling was murdered. And Biling had stood there for fifteen seconds watching while poor Derek Mountain got his brains scrambled in a test in Carl Robollo's lab. And Spotty had left the gala with Carl's daughter. What was the connection? She called up Simon, showed him Spotty's picture.

"It's a scummy face," he said. "Is he a welfnik?"

"It would explain the awful complexion, wouldn't it? This is from the Colosseum's sec record."

"Yes, I can see. You want I should try an ID?"

"And/or connections," Lavendar said.

"No problem."

"How are you going with the diversion package?"

"Almost ready."

"What's the angle?"

"Biling was done by organ snatchers."

Disgusting. Sometimes Simon's sense of the grotesque was too much. "Is that really necessary?"

"It has to be more sensational than a ringland connection, doesn't it? A diversion?" Grinning.

He was right, of course. Organ snatchers would do very well.

◊

The Ratman knows a lady, cool as glass. Oh, boy, oh boy. That lady has it, has it. Ratman can't escape, a slave. It does your bidding, Lady. It kisses your feet. It waits and watches for the Cool Eyes smile. It fights Froggy in the Marshes of the Moon. Even unto the Valley of the Shadow of Death, the Ratman drags its brain across the floor to please the lady. Lady frowns and Ratman trembles. Lady smiles and Ratman's blood is fighting through its head. And Ratman will tell it all, Lady, will write it down in the Truth that Knows. And when it's dead, the world will see. Ratman in love, Cabber. Ratman, poor Ratman.

Words, words, words, though. Just, just, just. Working at the bench on the neural translator. Had it sorted nearly, hooked it to the spare headset, extra probes to bone onto the skull direct. A standard interface like rub-a-dub, Robollo said, but a clever, clever program. Pretty program. Charlie, you will love this little program. Ratman is a Gee-Nee-Uss. You know that, Lady? See that, Lady, how your slave is? Never a queen had a cleverer slave. Poor Ratman.

Not now, though. No time for love now. Had to load it up and turn it on. The click switch, pretty power light glows green. It's green for go, Ratman. Go, go, go. And sent the code in from its desktop. See? A light still green. It's a-okay. So watch this, Lady, watch the Ratman run the first little test. I-I-I-I-I-I-I-I-I-it's WORKING! Maybe. Maybe, it's working, looks okay but hard to tell until you go in there and see. Or open the head up, let that all inside.

Put the headset on, the probes in through the hair. Lie

down now. Don't need the Optigene, don't need to stare. And turn it on again? Now? Scary. Can't do it. Might fry the brain. Might blow the circuits. Ratman in love, Lady. Never see Cool Eyes smile no more.

Do it?

Do it.

No. No way.

DO IT YOU YELLOW-BELLIED SUCKER!

Switch. Nothing. Blank'n blink'n dark. Where's the chip to talk?

– Hey, chip.

– This is your neural translator chip here. What is your password?

It WORKS! It's GO. The Ratman could be in with the brain hooked straight into the wall socket. Now!

No.

Go!

No, no. Enough. Enough for now, no further. Got to talk to Charlie. Got to let Charlie know. Got to ask what happens next.

◊

Biling's diary and phone record went back three months. She ran a directory search against all the numbers and began to work through them from the beginning. Not much to go on. Apart from calls to a couple of restaurants, a courier company, and an organisation that looked as if it dealt in computer software, Biling's only recorded telephone communications were with internal Galen numbers. All his listed appointments seemed to be work related as well. Further on she came to the name Candy's. Three times over a two-week period. Interesting. A place like that was way outside Biling's fashion league, surely, like the ZIG gala. And there was the software company again. Knoware Applications Design. Were they suppliers to Galen? Or did Biling have some connection with the computer industry outside his work?

She clicked her control to bring the last page of appointments and phone calls up on her wall vid. Immediately a name leapt out at her. Isis Image Management. For a moment, she couldn't take it in, just sat staring. How could it be? A mistake, surely. Four times in three days. What on earth was Biling doing calling... Who was he calling? And why?

She dialled up Simon.

"Have you spoken to anyone from Galen lately?"

"No. Should I have?" He looked puzzled.

"Frank Biling didn't call here?

"Biling? Good Lord, no."

"His phone record says he did."

"What? When?" Simon looked astonished now.

"There's been nothing recorded on the video mail?"

"Not from him."

"Very strange."

"Maybe Myerson or Robollo used his phone," Simon suggested.

"Why would they do that?" But perhaps he was right. There was no other explanation, was there? Unless it was a foul up, a coincidence, the records getting twisted somehow.

"Call and ask them," he suggested.

Yes, she thought, I will. In a moment. Maybe. Because something was stopping her. Something at the back of her mind, an idea which... Forget it, she told herself. It'll come to you when it's ready.

"How have you been getting on?" she asked. "Any progress?"

"Yes, actually." He gave one of his sly, pleased with himself grins. "Take a look."

A window opened with a shot of a grey concrete corridor, camera angle a little above head height. Then two men appeared, one tall and thin with blond hair, wearing a fawn-coloured three-piece suit, the other was Spotty Face. They were unsteady on their feet and laughing, drunk perhaps?

"Where on earth did you get this" Lavendar asked.

"You don't want to know. It's the Colosseum. Level BG 5

or 6. A few days ago. There isn't full camera coverage down there. This is the only shot we've got."

"Do you have an ID?" Lavendar asked.

"Not for our party. The tall one's called Friis (that's F-R-double-I-S) Blackstone but it seems it's an aka. Not a very savoury character."

Spotty Face was wearing, good heavens, a flower in his button hole. The two figures weaved out of camera range.

"What do you mean 'unsavoury'? Who is he?"

"An information dealer. On the shady side. Very few established connections except through what seems to be a phantom company called David Livid Enterprises."

"That's the name that Spotty mentioned at the gala. Must be our man."

"Maybe."

"Call Super Research and get them to do a full run down on Blackstone and David Livid and see if they can find any connections with Biling and Derek Mountain."

"Sure." Simon paused. His image looked at her curiously.

"Tell me," he said. "Why are we pushing this so hard?"

"Why?" It was obvious, wasn't it? But the question had disconcerted her.

"Isn't this getting a bit personal, Lavendar?"

"Personal? Of course, it's personal. Isis is on the line here." Snappy, she didn't need to snap at him. She took a big breath, smiled. Or tried to. "I don't know," she said. "I really don't know. Except that I feel I've been cheated somehow. There's something weird going on. Like those phone calls." And suddenly she understood.

Myerson had doctored the phone record, made it look as if Biling had called Isis. Why? Because if it came to light for some reason that the security video had been tampered with, what better explanation than that Biling had found his own image management company, one that Galen did not normally use, and had arranged the job himself? To hide his guilt. And Myerson, of course, was allowing her to see the record now as a warning. He probably guessed that she had kept a copy of the original security play and was simply pointing out to her how useless it was.

◊

Lying there in the wristic fuckin douse, jack, boring as a droppo convention with Jank and her sibs all goggling at the world go round, a pack of geeks. Spit here, like another geek, wondering at what the hell it mattered if he had a pocket full of clink, and folding clink, jack, couldn't use a fleck of it. He died rich, jack, and what the fuck good did it do him?

He stared at the room, the walls. It was different somehow. Lights had faded. It was all dim like a real time movie. Shit! A sudden hiss and two of the wall carpets shot up into the ceiling. Behind them was a big vid, as big as the one he'd seen that night, the brainjoy night, the Queen of Heaven. And the thought of it triggered him suddenly so he knew. This was the same place. Not exactly the same, but the same deal, jack, the same wristic, fuckin deal. He felt sick with excitement, anticipation, fear.

The black surface of the vid was glowing, there were two or three little points of brightness. Then, smoothly, quickly, the lights came in. A room, a huge room filled with techno-garbage, jack. There were screens and wires and boxes and things half made or half taken apart. A stack of coloured cartons, a scatter of abandoned boards in a corner, a long bench splayed with tools and monitors and meters and jumbled parts. It was a shambles, butcher blast of chaos, jack. And it was all live. Every screen was glowing with a picture or a whirling, graph of some or other kind. There were animals and people, bright cartoons and flickering forms, scrolling columns of numbers and symbols, scrambled static.

The nerve centre. This is the heart of the brain. And the brain of the heart. The thoughts came in from nowhere. Freaky, jack.

In the distance, in one corner, there was a movement, a figure. Someone in a wheelchair, Spit could see, was coming at him quick and looming, huge. It was there, it was charging! Fuck! He hid his head.

"Hello!" A voice boomed.

Spit looked up and saw the image in the wall was a round face, enormous, white, with sagging cheeks and thin red lips. It wore a black leather cap with silver studs around the band and a big, diamante butterfly in the middle of the peak. It had a black patch over the left eye.

"Hello there!" Grinning. It was freaky biz, though, too. Something on the lips. They might have blood on them.

"Ah, I'm too close, aren't I? Sorry." The image shifted, shrivelled. A dud in a wheelchair, a fat dud in the cap and a black leather jacket. Face white as flour. Mouth with a big grin. Spit knew this person, knew something about him. Or her. He was not quite sure.

"Allow me to introduce myself. Livid's the name. David Livid."

"Hello," Spit said. "Sir." He was a mush brain saying "sir", a full-out puke, but he couldn't help himself. The fat man was delighted.

"Lovely," he laughed. "Lovely, lovely. We've met before, Arlen. Do you remember?"

"Yer," Spit said. He was trying to remember.

Livid lifted his hand and hooked his fingernails into claws. Then he laughed again and showed a double row of blackened teeth. "The Queen of Heaven! You remember very well, I know. And now you've come to see me. To help me. Yes?"

"Yes," Spit said. There was nothing else to say.

"And something else, too. You had something of mine. You lost it, didn't you?" Livid stared, grinning, kept on staring. And Spit remembered the little blue box with the thing inside. Livid winked the eye without the patch. And then, suddenly, Spit figged it. Fuck, that patch! The eye! No, jack, it couldn't be. No, no.

Livid watched him feeling it and grinned, raised his hand very slowly to the eye-patch and suddenly whipped it off. Spit twisted away, couldn't bear it, couldn't bear to see.

"Bouncy! Bouncy! Bouncy!"

Spit looked up and fuck it, jack, there were two good eyes staring at him out of the fat face in the wall.

"Tricked you!" Livid laughed.

PART THREE

into the hard

14

Hospital Denies Gutting Connection!

Caduceus Transplant Clinic today denied any connection with the gang of organ snatchers said to be roaming the city. Spokesperson Wanda Frippley said the suggestion was 'preposterous'. 'Caduceus has never had any problem sourcing suitable donors. To think that we would need to stoop to such depravities would be laughable if the idea were not so appalling.' Speculation about an illegal trade in human organs has been mounting since the gutted body of Frank Biling, Medical Technician, was found in a Thorndon alley last night. PNPC investigators deny any evidence of organ snatcher involvement but crimestrend observers point out that there is no other obvious explanation for this ghastly crime.

Channel 29 Newsbase

– **C**harlie? Hey, Charlie. Ratman got one for you. Boy, oh, boy.

– Steady on, son. Play it cool there.

– Cool as a pool as a rule.

– What you got?

– I got the hardware, Charlie. You know, little neural nudger.

– It works?

– It talks to Ratman. Little chip say 'hi there, you want to come in?'

– You go in?

– Not yet, Charlie. Ratman scared. A bit. Not knowing what.

– Yer, I know. And you be careful, boy. I don't want you doin' no damn fool thing.

– Ratman, okay. Ratman want to play. To work. You know. Give it a hard problem, Charlie. You know. A really, really. Everything you got too easy.

– Stay cool, boy. And don't you use that thing you invented.

– Work, work, work, Charlie. Now, now, now.

– Stay cool there. Just give me the specs and the code and…

– No, no, no. Tradey, trade, trade, Charlie. You want the goodies, you give Ratman something. Bit of fun for the genius boy. Gee-Nee-Uss. You know, Charlie.

– Okay, okay. I'll go looking. I got a couple of things lining up. And I got some new research in the pipeline. I'll get you a package.

– Big package, Charlie. Bee-ee-ee-ee-g package. Better, better, better be.

– Just hold on there.

◊

Spit on his back on a couch in a little room behind the office. Staring up at the ceiling, jack, the blank white space like an empty vid with all the world to come on it. A wristic fuckin wonderland and no mistake, jack, racy little SKB. Because Blyss wasn't around and there were no runs to do.

So what the fuck? An ASP was never bored. An ASP had all his own resources. Boredom was a failure of the spirit, lack of imagination. So show your power, jack.

> V is for violence to beat out the truth
> A for aggression to drive to the goal
> C for confession, the victim gives in
> U for unbounded, the power and the glory
> U for unbounded, restraint all abandoned
> M for the meaning whose birth is in action

And that was touch, jack. That was red nails in the flesh. It was glow and fire and worth and two unboundeds in an emphasis. He liked the two unboundeds, a kind of poetry (not that he gave a shit except for some of the stuff in the *One Thousand Great Lines of Verse* he'd read for his English Lit credits).

He sat up suddenly, stood up. Found out then how stiff he was. Just lying on your back, jack. Fucks the soul. So why not? Nobody said he had to lie there doing nothing. All Blyss said was to be discreet, or some other wristic bloody word. He opened the door, walked down the corridor into the office. Empty. Blyss was out there, doing it. Blyss had other offices, other deals, Spit knew. He had biz nobody knew about and all tied up with the fat freak Livid in the wheelchair. Spit still couldn't fig if Livid was the Queen of Heaven or just some wrister who knew that slam. Shit, what a weirdo, jack! And all that gear. It looked like Livid was a technofreak of no mean proportion. And he was the Boss, jack. Spit had no doubt about that.

He sat at the desk, swung himself around and back a few times in Blyss's chair.

Thought of Calliope. A charming young lady with an array of glorious talents. Well, why not? He dialled the number.

And shit, jack, he was lucky. Calliope answered, looked at him. Grinned when she saw who it was. A real nice smile.

"Hi, there, sister," he said.

"How're you going?" she asked.

"Sweet. And you?"

"They grounded me. You know for the other night. Embarrassing them and leaving with you. Bringing you back here."

"I'm persona non whatever, right?"

"Right, jack." She grinned some more.

"Tough," he said. "You know, I think you're slick. You got touch. I guess... you know. You got pissed and so forth but I had a real nice time."

"Even when I threw up?"

"Well, you know. It happens, jack. How long they ground you for?"

"A week."

"Heavy shit!"

"It's okay. Only five to go. When it's over, maybe we could get together."

"Sure. That be sweet, jack."

"There's one freaky thing, though." She looked worried all of a sudden, two line creases between her eyes. "That dud we spoke to the other night. The one you knew, Frank Biling?"

"Yer."

"He's dead. Somebody killed him. Right after the gala by the look of it."

"Hey!" Heavy shit, jack! Killed him? Like Tobin? "That's tough," he said.

"Everybody here's..." Suddenly the screen went blank. Nothing. Nothing but the hum of the dial tone. He called back and got what he expected. The bald-headed butcher with the bloodshot eyes and the warty ear.

"Listen, cocksucker," it said. "Just piss..."

Spit cut it off before it had a chance to finish.

So they were listening, jack. They knew. And Blyss wanted him to get alongside Calliope. And Biling was dead. It was freak, jack, but he felt no panic, not much anyway. A kind of calm. Thinking about it. Something, something going down he didn't fig.

He was still thinking about it when Blyss arrived.

"Well, good morning, then," Blyss said. "I've got a little job for you."

◊

There was a message from Mark Bullington and another from Curtis Caid. Just at the moment, though, she didn't really care about either of them. She suddenly wanted to be in touch with her family, really missed them. Strange how that could happen, such a strong feeling of need. She flicked into the mail system and set up a message to her parents in their Padua hotel.

"Hello Darlings, I hope you're having a fabulous time over there and not working too hard. I'm frantically busy at the moment with a terrible case which I can't tell you about but something is going on with one of my clients and everyone's running around trying to sort out the mess. Like fleas in a fit as you might say, Daddy. Anyway, this is just a quick one to let you know I'm thinking about you. Lots of love, now. Bye."

And she felt just a little sad when she'd sent it, just a little lonely. She wanted to spend more time with Cynthia, give Madeleine all the new insights she had recently had into her sister's character. She wanted to hear about Cynthia's latest fertility treatment and whether or not she'd ever thought about that cloning thing that Madeleine had mentioned, IUC was it called? And about Cynthia's husband who... Good Lord! She hadn't even properly realised that Cynthia would have a husband. Wasn't that strange? What was he like? What was his name? Gerald? Yes, she thought so. Gerald. He would be tall and rangy, lean, with a moustache and blue eyes. Eyelids just a little wrinkled from squinting into the sun. An outdoors sort of person, the sort of person who... Careful, she thought, careful.

A window opened in the left-hand lower corner of the wall vid and a face appeared. Short blond hair and brown eyebrows, carefully chiselled lips. Androgynous. One of the simulated fronts for Super Research, the confidential investigation company she and Simon used.

"Good morning, Ms Tempest. We have some information for you."

"Thank you," she said, dragging her mind back to the problems of her working life and grateful, perhaps, to be brought back to earth.

A second window opened next to the face and a skein of words began to roll slowly down it.

Name: Frickstone Blyss
  aka Friis Blackstone
  aka Buck Freestone

Address: Unstable
Place of Birth: Unknown
Age: Uncertain
Listed Occupation: Information Broker
Unlisted activities: software piracy
 information espionage
 suspected tax evasion
 suspected CBF
 suspected welfare fraud

Known associates: David Livid (HS)

No criminal record

"Not much to go on," Lavendar said. "Seems like one elusive character."

The face didn't answer. Her comment was obviously too phatic for its taste.

"No links with Frank Biling or Carl Robollo?"

"Not that we can determine."

Lavendar stared at the block of words, trying to fathom where the secret was.

"What does HS mean after Livid's name?"

"Hearsay."

"Even more elusive than Blyss."

"We have very little evidence that this person exists at all. No visuals, no demographics," the face said.

"And did you find out if either of them knows Derek Mountain?"

"Mountain works for a company called Casturian System Development. No connection with Blyss or Livid that we have determined."

"He's a technology person?"

"Yes."

"Like Robollo. Is that a coincidence?"

Again the face didn't respond. It had no opinion on coincidences.

It was the only common thread, though. Mountain and

Robollo were both computer buffs and Blyss was involved in software piracy. And Biling was Robollo's friend supposedly and also...

"Are any of these people connected with a company called Knoware Applications Design?"

"Just one moment, we will check." The face stared at her, impassive, while the system behind it made an enquiry on its databases. After a few seconds, it gave a little twitch and its regular friendly smile. "Knoware officially ceased business five days ago," it said. "Shareholders were, however, listed as Frank Biling and David Livid."

Yes!

"So Biling knew Livid?"

"It would seem so."

"Even though you said Livid didn't exist."

"We have little evidence of existence."

"So who else is linked with Knoware? Any employees?"

"We have no names listed."

"A phantom company?"

"It would seem so. It may have been set up to hold software patents. That is a common practice."

"I have a telephone number, though. Biling called them."

"We think you will find that has been disconnected."

So, still nothing to go on. No people to talk to. Except Robollo, who was part of Galen and probably couldn't be trusted.

"No leads you can give me then," she said.

"We have visuals from our Suspicious Persons Tracking System. Blyss has been sighted at several points around the city. Cardoman, The Downtowner, Candy's, several levels of the Colosseum."

Candy's again. She sat there, thinking, feeling. A strange sense of anxiety. Because these people were dangerous, almost certainly. Frank Biling's death and his weird behaviour before it were just the beginning, the tiny visible sign of something hidden and horrible, like those awful stories about skin cancer. Impossible to know how deep or wide it was. And yet if she didn't approach it, didn't do all she could to find it and destroy it, she ran the risk of being betrayed by Galen and being dragged into it anyway. She had no choice, therefore. She had to act, had to be urgent and energetic and purposeful. For the moment, though, she didn't, couldn't move. Just sat there. Didn't even notice when the simul timed out and signed off, to be replaced by a picture of Michaelangelo's *David*. She just sat staring. Thinking about nothing much. Thinking, perhaps, about Cynthia and her husband on their Hawkes Bay farm and how nice it would be to ride a horse through the morning dew.

15

I'm a silly, silly,
Bumble, bumble,
Mumble kind of man
But I love you.
Yes, I love you
Like no other fella can.
So let's get a place together
In a quiet part of town
And we'll sit and watch the telly
As the evening sun goes down.

Scott Scott of The Bland Brothers

Rain. This run was a pisser, jack. A bar on the waterfront, a slink called Casey. She would be sitting at a table by the window and smoking coloured cigarettes. Down out of the tubestreet and across the overway. The bar was in a drive-up complex and no way to it except across the open space with the wind ripping at you. SKB. He waited for the rain to ease and then made a dash for it, his new shoes pounding in the puddles, ducked into the shelter of a carpark entrance, jumped aside as a Panther Sports came through and nearly bowled him, wristic fucking butcher, jack.

He straightened his cuffs and his lapels and set off walking, echoes on the cold concrete. The Panther was parked a couple of rows down and a tall dud getting out, short cut green hair and he was slim, jack, in a slick suit, sense of touch. Spit took the steps in double time, a corridor and out into the complex.

He could see the concourse through the glass doors at the end. But then. He stopped. Leaning against the wall beside the glass door, looking cool but keeping out of sight, was a big dud, a suit, with dark face, black hair. Turbo butcher, made Spit nervous.

A noise behind. He half-turned to see the green-haired dud, coming up the steps, looking slick with his hand in his jacket pocket. And then big dud started moving and Spit suddenly felt the squeeze. The two of them, they had a double drop on him. The corridor was concrete, walls and floor, and two metres wide maybe. Which way? He started walking towards the big dud, taking it easy, like he had his own biz, jack, and wasn't scuffed by nobody. And moving towards the wall on his left, to walk on smoothly past. The dud changed his angle too, to narrow down the gap, which was good, jack, just the way. They were getting closer now and he could feel Green Hair behind him, sense the distance, not too far. And then.

Spit took off, cutting to his right where the big gap was and seeing the big dud coming at him, ran for it, and the big arms opening at him, Spit, with a quick slash, hit him across the face with the carry on its safety cord, a swinging clunk. And he was out towards the glass door, with Green Hair yelling at him. Shooter. There was a shooter, he could feel it. Cringing for the shot, which didn't come. And he was free. He was out free, out in the crowd and walking quickly, one of all these people, happy, jack, and smiling at a geri with a shopping basket. He saw the bar over to his right but he wasn't making any moves on that, jack, no kidoda. And what was the point. The cord from the carry was dangling from his wrist with nothing on the end. And hope to shit that dataslice was wiped like Blyss had said it would be.

◊

Nothing, nothing, nothing. Still no nothing. Froggy was a clever one. Froggy knew the trap was there, maybe. Kept out of the way. And Ratman watching, itching. Brain was wriggly, wouldn't stop. A jumpy, jumpy brain or running like a cockroach up and down and round and round and Charlie didn't come 'cos Charlie was a meany. Ratman walking. Up and down and round and round and hit the walls. The Ratman hit the walls with his fist but it did no good, the itchy brain was getting bad, bad, bad and mad, mad, mad. So get on the network, then. But that no good. For sure thing Ratman look for Charlie go all a-begging. Please, Charlie, please, a hard one please. And Charlie saying no to punish or saying yes, you give me all the specs, the code and then I'll see. Starving the Ratman, punishing and twisting. No, not fair.

And where was Cool Eyes? Not fair, neither. Queen too busy for a poor slave. Think of her, though. Just think. A Ratman might. And maybe that was better, how she smiled.

So the Ratman sat down at the workbench and it started to write.

> *Oh, Cool Eyes, Queen.*
> *The Mistress of the Day*
> *Your smile is like the Silver Stars*
> *Your Brain is like the Genius of Heaven*
> *You are the Ratman's Wonder*
> *You are the Ratman's Secret Soul*
> *Without you it is Just an Insect*
> *Cockroach Ratman*
> *Crushed like a Crunchy by Your Lovely Foot*
> *Oh Ratman Worship*
> *Ratman Love*
> *And All the Clever Puzzles of a Thousand Years*
> *The Ratman lay its Brain beneath your Feet*
> *For You to Step on*
> *Never had a Day, Poor Ratman*
> *Never had a Hope.*
> *So Love*
> *So Help Me.*

Didn't even look but sent it.

◊

She was with Curtis. At Candy's. He had called, in what seemed to be a spontaneous gesture, and asked her if she could do lunch and she had thought, why not? Especially when she could suggest the venue and take the opportunity of looking around. Curtis, for his part, wanted to celebrate. It seemed he had been promoted. Personal assistant to Carol Carlion. Quite close to Edmond Eliades, when you thought about it. Strange, that only a few days ago such news would have really interested her whereas now she felt quite detached from it. There was no point in giving any thought to minor things until the main problem of her life was solved. And solve it she would, she was sure. Perhaps even today.

Delicately, she speared a slice of apple and chewed on it. Tasted the tart and juicy sweetness round her tongue. Curtis was talking about the system failures around the city; the strange things that had been happening to network performance and the corruptions to on-line movies and TV broadcasts.

"Have you had anything of the sort?" he asked her.

"No, not really. But then I don't really watch TV very much."

"Oh, TV's the least of it!" He threw up his hands in disgust. "It's the impact on one's work environment that I can't stand. I mean sometimes it takes half an hour to get the simplest report across town. A courier would be quicker. Carol's onto it, of course. It's her big thrust at the moment. Alongside this tax reform plan is a complete systems revamp. And my bet is, she'll get her way."

Major changes, upheaval, announcements, media requirements; Lavendar could imagine the scale of it, the need for people who were skilled at getting the message across in exactly the right way. And wasn't Curtis here now precisely to present her with the opportunity? Ironic, she thought, that I can't pursue it. Not yet.

"I mean," Curtis said, "the sense of frustration in the

population at large. These Combined Council inefficiencies. It's unbelievable. You must have seen it."

"An ideal media moment for a revolution."

"Exactly. And Carol's right there, on the spot. Right in Edmond's eye."

In his eye? What did that mean exactly? She imagined the people closest to the great man: his friends, his advisers, his lovers. Who were they? Edmond Eliades, she realised, had always managed to avoid the scandals which the media seemed to drum up about other members of the power elite.

"Edmond isn't married, is he? Does he have any special friends?" she asked.

"Special?" Curtis looked puzzled for a moment and then laughed. "Oh, no, no. He believes in chastity. It's a teaching he follows. Sexual energy should be directed towards creative goals. For the betterment of business."

"Is that Eastern?"

"No. From Dannevirke. The Church for the Advancement of Personal Destiny. Edmond likes all his closest staff to belong to it."

He started to explain and Lavendar sat in a position that indicated attention. She stopped listening after a few moments, though. Curtis's enthusiasm for religion was one of his least endearing traits. He seemed to have this fascination for doctrine as if it embodied a kind of truth instead of merely being what some people believed. She did wonder for a moment what his interest in this particular set of ideas meant for their relationship but put the complication, if it was a complication, from her mind. There were more important things to consider just now.

As she nodded and smiled, she let her peripheral vision drift over the nearby tables. Looking for someone, of course. No reason to believe that he would be here, no reason to think she would spot him if he were. Candy's was a big place and carefully designed so that there were always corners where one could be discreet. Except that she had a sense somehow. Her instinct told her. Today. Here. Now.

"That sounds absolutely fascinating," she said. "Can an ordinary person join?"

Curtis looked startled at the interruption. "I don't know. You'd have to talk to Morton Crayne."

"Who's he?"

"He heads the whole thing up."

"Edmond's guru?"

"Yes, I suppose you could say that."

"And there's no sex at all?"

"Absolutely not."

And maybe it wouldn't be such a bad thing. Cleansing, somehow. Focusing. She could imagine, though, what Daddy would say. Scornful, oh, yes, that was certainly the word.

"If you'll excuse me for a moment." She smiled at him, stood up. Walked away, down the steps towards the beachfront. The sky was a soft warm blue and there were several simulations of yachts out there. The beachfront tables were tucked away in little alcoves of bushes, soft pink flowers, oleanders were they? People at them talking, one or two alone. And he was here, she was certain. How did she know? It wasn't logical to be so sure. It was probably quite arrogant, but then... A couple sitting holding hands. The man looked up at her as she passed. She felt the brief touch of his eyes. She turned left, up a flight of wide steps. Couldn't be away from Curtis too long, could she?

He was sitting at a table beside a vine-covered wall. He had another man with him, an oldish fellow with silver hair, but handsome, in his way. She moved towards them slowly, putting something just a little extra into her walk, waiting for them to notice. The older one looked up first. A thin, lined face but tanned. Blue eyes. She didn't look at him, though. Kept her gaze on Blyss, felt the older one staring at her and watched as Blyss realised, turned, looked at her with eyebrows raised, round, looping eyebrows like a clown.

She went right up to him. He tried to stand up, do the gallant thing but she was already too close and crowded him back into his seat.

"Mr Blyss?" She held out her hand. He took it, cold, thin fingers. For a moment, she thought he was going to kiss the back of her wrist, but he let her go after a brief, soft clasp.

"Dear lady," he said, grinning. Thin lips, wide mouth, like his mouth and his eyebrows were all part of a big circle.

"My name's Lavendar Tempest, Isis Image Management. One of my clients is Galen Corporation." She sensed a quick movement from the other man, anxiety, perhaps, but she kept her eyes on Blyss, gave him her card. "I think we need to talk. To our mutual advantage, I hope."

"Really? Hmmm." He looked at her, still grinning, with his head on one side. Like a big bird.

"Call me," she said. "This afternoon." She turned away. They watched her, she felt it, all the way across the patio.

◊

Spit sat in the office waiting for Blyss to come back. Sat, jack? Fiddled around, walked up and down. Trying to fig it. The big dud and Green Hair. With a shooter, maybe. At the time, when it was happening, he'd felt slick and cool but now he had a freak on, jack. It was no fuckin good. It was NFG. Better off at home, better off with Jank and her mates, better off with telly and the FAM.

You reck?

He stopped, breathed hard. One breath in and let it out. Another. Control, he told himself. An ASP is always in control. Of the inner world at least. But a shooter? That was heavy time. That was big load. And Biling, and the associate, they was done too. Blyss and Livid weren't so cosy, maybe. Things were closing in.

Cellphone started to burr. Spit flicked it open and pressed the in call button. The little screen filled with a face, a pale face with black hair. Calliope.

"Spit?"

He pressed the out call so she could see him.

"Spit, I can't talk. They're after me. They want to get me."

Her, too? Hey, jack, wait. This was weirdo stuff. This was...

"I ran away," she went on. "I'm in... I'm in the Colosseum. Can you meet me?" Her eyes big, white face, red lips twisted like she was going to do that crying shit. So, what to do?

"Where are you, jack?"

"I'm in the old bit, the grotty bit. Floor six. There's a bar here at the north end. Ratz, it's called. R-A-T-Z."

He knew it, knew the area. Was safe enough?

"Who after you, jack? A green hair?"

"Green? No. Don't know. Just a guy. They... Look, I can't talk now. Okay?"

"Okay. I'll be there. Wait for me. Don't move."

He hung up, went to stand up but then thought, no, hey, what a minute, jack. What the fuck was he doing? There were duds out there with shooters prowling around. There was the Mole and whoever did Tobin's associate. And the butchers who did Biling, too. Waiting for him, any one of them. Why expose himself? Why go out there just because some bird he'd met was in a freak? Leave her, he told himself. To hell with Blyss and the glorious talents. An ASP looked after number one.

16

Fashion! Fashion! Fashion!

Big Parade offers you more choice at cheaper prices.

Take advantage of our state of the art design system.

Every outfit guaranteed different.

Hutt Woman's Weekly

Scrit, scrit, scrit. Scrat, scrat, scrat. Itchy, bitchy Ratman. Ratman take a shower, maybe. All the wetty water, witty water. Witty and pity and city. Ratman didn't like it, though. Not that wetting, petting, creepy. Creepy water made its skin crawl, creep. And made it itchy more.

So Ratman sat at the workbench, work. With the hands on the keyboard, staring at the screen. Watching for Froggy. But Froggy wouldn't come. All the little itsy-bitsy figures come rolling down the screen with all the okey-dokey, all okay. Stats from other places told where Froggy was. And weird. All weird and wired. Because Froggy had some cunning ways and seemed to disappear and reappear. Like it was not a roly-poly, only like a ball, but also nothing. Like water, creepy water, flowing out through all the little cracks and coming back together in another place. How you do that, Froggy? How do you know how to trickle through the trap? A clever, clever. Ratman get you, though. The Ratman got the brain, you bet.

Flicker to its right. The vid phone screen. And there she

was. The Ratman's Queen. And how its heart went crazy pumping. Oh, oh, oh.

"Good morning, Mr Pope." Not smiling, no, no, no. And all about the poor Ratman's poem maybe. Turn on the vision? It couldn't, wouldn't. Too, too, too, too, too....

Queen kept talking. "I guess you're there, because you usually are. And it probably doesn't matter if you're hiding...." Ratman ducked its head down to its arms, looked at her sideways, side angle. "I just want to acknowledge your message, your... whatever it was..." Poem, lady, poem. Ratman wrote a poem for his Queen. "Maybe I should be flattered about something like that but I suppose my main reaction is concern. We have a business relationship here. A business problem. And to be quite honest, if it doesn't get solved pretty damn quick, the consequences for everyone involved will be quite serious." Ratman trying, lady. Ratman really, really, really... "So I guess my only message to you is that I have already started looking for alternative ways to a solution. If you can't get focused on the main issue and give me an answer within twenty-four hours, then I will be contacting Charlie Cato and asking for you to be removed from the case. Understand?"

No, no, no, not Charlie. No, no, no. 'Cos Charlie will be nasty. Charlie will be mad and do... And what will Ratman do without its Queen? So, pleeeeaase. Don't worry, lady. Ratman find a way. For Ratman know, and go, and flow. The fine flow lady. Yes, yes, yes. It'll get you Froggy. Froggy on a plate.

◊

"Thank you," Lavendar said. "I'm sure we'll get along fine now."

Madeleine Drummond smiled a little nervously. "You should perhaps understand that Cynthia might not be all that natural in her responses. And she might also be rather passive. She has so little background at the moment."

"Yes, I do understand that."

"Fine. Anything you need, then, just let me know."

Lavendar sat looking at her sister's image. Cynthia gazed back at her with an expression of gentle sadness. Such a sweet face, really lovely with its look of natural health and just that little touch of tragedy about the eyes. It was easy to see the family resemblance and to realise too that Cynthia was the elder by five years. I might grow to look like that, Lavendar thought, if my bone structure was broader and I was subject to the country life.

"I don't really have long to talk," Lavendar said, "just a few moments, but I couldn't resist spending them with you."

"That's really nice," Cynthia answered.

"How are things down there in the country?"

"Fine. Just fine."

"And how's Gerald?"

Cynthia didn't answer.

"Your husband Gerald, how is he?"

"Oh, Gerald. He's fine too."

"Working hard as usual?"

"You know Gerald," Cynthia said.

"How long have you two been married now?"

"Two months?" Cynthia suggested.

"No, no. Much longer than that. Twelve years, isn't it?"

"Twelve years. Yes, that's right."

"February the fourteenth. I remember your wedding so well. I was really quite jealous, you know."

"Jealous? Why?"

"Oh, I guess I was young and silly. Head full of romantic nonsense. I thought getting married must be the most wonderful thing in the world."

"It's not all it's cracked up to be, you know," Cynthia said.

"I know that *now*, of course."

"Gerald is a lovely man but he does work hard. Always working. Sometimes I think I hardly have a husband. Not that I'm complaining mind you."

"The farm must take a lot of work. I know you work hard too."

"Oh, yes. But then it helps to take my mind off things."

"Yes, well, how is it going with all that?"

"Well, I had an appointment with Dr Dickinstone in Napier yesterday. It seems there's absolutely no reason why I can't have a baby with these new in vitro or cloning techniques. They can virtually guarantee success these days. But, then, driving back here and looking at all the trees and the flowers along the roadside near the beautification project, I really wondered if, you know, if it wasn't somehow wrong to go against nature. I mean, if I was meant to have a child, I would have one, wouldn't I? And perhaps it's wiser not to struggle against one's destiny."

Ah, yes, Lavendar thought. This sounds more like Cynthia.

"What does Gerald think?" she asked.

"Gerald? Oh, my husband. I see what you mean. Well, he would think something I suppose, wouldn't he?"

"Perhaps you should ask him."

"Perhaps I should."

"You have to work it out together."

"Yes, we do, don't we?"

"And Gerald's such an understanding man. Considerate. You've always said so."

"Yes, I have, haven't I?"

"He may agree with you, of course. Or he may take a different point of view."

"That's what's going to be interesting, isn't it?"

Cynthia smiled the same sad smile. Then her look brightened suddenly and she said, "And how are you getting on? How are all those really difficult projects?"

"Oh, making progress, I think. But I have to be a little careful."

"Oh, why's that?"

"There's a certain criminal element involved in some of it."

"Well, you should probably go to the police."

"Yes, you're right."

"Let people do the jobs they're paid to do," Cynthia said.

"I mean, I don't chase criminals down here on the farm. And neither does Gerald. There are other people to do that."

"You're probably right. It's hard to give up an interesting and exciting project, though."

"I'll send you some flowers. We have lovely spring flowers here already. Daffodils and jonquils and..." But then, suddenly, her face froze. And started to change. Swelling, the cheeks growing fat and pale, the eyes screwing up into tight little wrinkles. Her hair disappeared, leaving only a handful of lank strands round the fringe of a skull covered with flaky skin. Her mouth grew wide, the lips slack and red, and hanging open stupidly to reveal stumps of blackened teeth. In seconds she had become a monster, disgusting, the most awful, awful...

"Gerald fucks a pig," she said. "Me!" And she gave a horrible, maniacal laugh.

Lavendar was already reaching out, switching into the call to Madeleine Drummond, when the Cynthia monster disappeared and Madeleine herself came on screen.

"Lavendar, oh, please. I am sorry! How can I apologise enough! These things, you know, they're starting to happen more and more frequently. It's some kind of horrible interference."

"Horrible isn't the word for it. It was ghastly, awful, unbelievably revolting. I have to take this to someone."

"Someone?" Madeleine stared at her as if she didn't understand. Or was it just naked fear? Good, Lavendar thought. Let her squirm. Someone has to suffer for poor Cynthia.

"What exactly happened?" she demanded.

"It's interference. Something from outside gets into our network. It's a kind of overloading apparently. Nobody can figure out exactly what it is."

Overloading? From outside? The words made a connection. She tried to think, but then became aware of the anxious, pitiful look on Madeleine's face. Poor woman, she thought. It isn't really her fault, is it?

"I won't say I'm happy, Madeleine, but I think I understand. There's really just one thing that concerns me. Is everything wasted? Is there going to be any permanent damage?"

"Oh, no. Most unlikely. I'm sure Cynthia will be fine and nothing you've done to date will be lost."

"Good. Fine. Perhaps, though, you could just actually check on that for me. Just to make sure."

"Certainly. Yes, of course."

"Good-bye." She turned Madeleine off and cut the conversation short, sat staring at her background image. Sun outside now. Rain had all gone suddenly, as if the weather was mocking her anger. A ghastly joke. And it was like a joke, wasn't it? Some awful crude piece of humour like drawing moustaches on things. And yet Madeleine said it was caused by a system fault. Network problem. A surge of input from outside. Myerson's words, weren't they? About the ENAS test. So what if someone had played exactly this sort of joke on poor Derek Mountain. Done something awful to his mental reality. What if Biling knew what was going on, somehow, or had engineered it? And yet, according to Curtis, these problems were happening all over the city. As if everyone was being threatened by the same thing.

You're paranoid, she told herself. And maybe she was. One thing was certain, though, whatever happened, someone was going to pay.

◊

Lay down, down, down with its head tilted back, with its arms along the side. New model headset was a neat fit, bit. So okay, Cool Eyes. See the Ratman. See it do the deed. You bet.

– Hey, chip. You there?

– This is your neural translator chip here. What is your password?

– Me. The Ratman.

– Repeat, please.

– Me. The Ratman.

– Hello, Ratman. This is your neural translator control

chip here. You will require an abort signal in case you wish to leave this network session in an emergency. What is your signal?

– Abort.

– Acknowledge. Abort, is that correct?

– Yes.

– Acknowledge. Please wait for your entry.

Wait, the gate. And eyes all blurry, blurry. Smeary lights through the Optigene and waiting for the video blat. Come on, come on, come on, chip. Ratman in a hurry, baby. Neural pads were throbbing, live things, wriggle. And then the Ratman was in, with the stuff coming at him, like genflak, like it always did but slower, oh, so slow. The coloured stuff like shear effect, lines of organ trace, green and blue like scuffmarks in a corridor. So what to do, man? Wait? So what's the difference? Receiving is transmitting, transmitting is going.

– Froggy? You out there Froggy. This is Ratman here. You seen the code, eh, Froggy. You know the Ratman's after you.

Watched it go, the message. Floating out and off and away. Sent it off to the node where the trap was. Froggy watch the trap, then Froggy know.

So, Queen. The Ratman here for you and fuck you, Charlie. Wait and see.

◊

The sixth floor of the Colosseum was a dump compared to the rest. It reminded him of home, the welfpark. Looked like it had been several big rooms once, like the place they'd held the gala, but now all that space had been chopped up with partitions into long twisting corridors of little shops and offices. Good place to hide, jack, filled with a jostling crowd of welfs and geris picking over the piles of crap that were on sale or huddling for warmth in the corners, nobody to know you here. And safe enough too with a security camera in every angle watching for the smallest sign of trouble.

Ratz was a square room with fake wooden panelling and

smoke-bleared photographs of foreign places. A bar in one corner and, above it, a big TV screen with a banjax game in progress. A bunch of duds in scruffy jackets and sweaters with holes in the elbows were huddled round the screen, peering up at it.

At first, Spit thought there was no one else in the place until he noticed a figure on the far side of the room, slouched in a chair which was jammed behind a Kings terminal. Calliope, with white face and dark eye make-up, hair hanging in drooping spikes over her forehead. Looked right on with the welfkids in the street outside.

"Hi, sister," Spit said, slipping into a chair beside her.

"They're after me," Calliope said, eyes big. She had a freak on for sure.

"Who, jack?"

"I don't know. It's my fault, I guess but I got sick of hanging around there, doing nothing. I couldn't call my friends. I wasn't allowed to do anything. And there was no reason. I mean, we didn't get into real trouble that night, did we? Fuck them, really. So I got to doing stupid things. Because I was bored, I guess. There was this thing came in the mail. A packet addressed to my father. And I knew what it was; I don't know how I knew but I did, somehow. Like I was looking for it, in a way. So I took it and I unwrapped it and I was right, it was a datablock, one of those hand held ones but with a little vid on it, and I fired it up and the face that fired up was this guy. And he said something like good evening, Mr Robollo, I hear one of your associates met with an accident, most unfortunate, and how he was calling to convey his condolences and he looked forward to meeting to discuss the implications. It didn't make any sense, not really, but I knew what it meant."

There was a sudden noise from the crowd by the bar, a burst of yelling and cheering, incredulous. "Hey, hey, hey, look at that," a voice yelled above the rest.

Calliope stared at the men. "One of those guys is watching me," she said.

Spit looked too. None of the duds over there seemed to be

interested in anything but the screen and slapping each other on the shoulder like real sporting wristers.

"So what happened with the block?" Spit asked.

"I tried to wrap it up again. But it was hard. There was a seal I hadn't noticed and I'd broken it. The next day my father called me into his study and showed me the thing. He didn't accuse me or anything. He just said, 'I don't know anything about the message on here and neither do you. Understand? It's got nothing to do with me and it's got nothing to do with you.' He was scared. I could tell. And I kind of believed him in a way. I wanted him not to be involved, you know? But then the guy arrived."

"Who?"

"I don't know his name. He came to the house. He saw me and I saw him and we knew. We both knew."

"When was this?" Spit asked.

"Today. This morning. That's when I panicked. I just ran. I got out of the place and came down here. They followed me."

"Who?"

"A big dark guy with a black beard. With a plate in his jaw." Calliope touched the left side of her face. The Kaiser, shit, this wasn't good, jack. "And another one," she went on. "He's over there by the bar."

Spit looked again.

"The one with the stupid hat," Calliope said. A weedy dud with a dirty woollen hat pulled down almost over his ears. It had a red pom-pom on top. His eyes were fixed on the TV screen which was running a commercial for the Catholic Church or some such crap. Staring at him didn't seem to faze the dud one bit but it had got the barman's attention. He was coming over. Another skinny dud, small, with a black moustache. He had a beat up metal tray in his hands.

"You folks want something?" he asked, giving the word 'folks' a special twist, the sarc of a hard done butcher, someone who sucked on the welfs and nonnos.

"Two sodas," Spit said.

"Nagh," said the barman. "More than that. Bottle of scotch maybe."

"We don't want scotch, jack."

"You sit here soaking up my heat, you buy my fuckin' scotch, mate."

"Your heat? I thought it came free with the building, jack."

"Everything here I own," he said, grinning. "Everything in this room that doesn't fart belongs to me." He grinned even more. "Come to think of it, your friend don't look she could raise any wind so maybe that includes her, eh?" And he laughed.

Spit turned to Calliope. "Come on, jack. Let's go."

Together out in the street. Spit glanced back and saw the guy with the hat come out of the bar. He grabbed Calliope's arm and they turned left down a narrow alley. A crowd of people moving both ways, jostling and pushing against each other, dumb ords trying to get through.

"That's him!" Calliope said, suddenly, pointing up ahead. A big, dark butcher, taller than the crowd, his shoulders like they were paddles, right and left. The Kaiser, sure. A black beard, a glint of brass as he swung his head.

"Here!" Calliope turned aside, dragging Spit into a smaller, narrower alley. There were fewer people. They could almost run. Another corner. The two duds both behind them now, moving as fast as they dared with the security cameras on them; couldn't make it obvious, a pattern of disturbance would trigger an automatic alert.

The corridor came to a T-junction. What to do, jack? Left along a dingy passage. Right, a shorter one with light at the end. They went right, running now, a few more metres and out into an open, empty space. A lift lobby. Standing there, waiting, waiting for the lift to arrive with the two butchers coming at them down the passage. Spit ran to a point in front of one of the corner cameras and jumped up and down, pointing.

"Hey!" he yelled. "Help! They're after us! Look! Look!"

"Come on!" Calliope was already in one of the lifts

waiting. Spit after her. The doors closed as the Kaiser arrived outside. He made like a dog with his teeth, reaching out with his arm to get it into the narrowing gap, but he was too slow. The thump, thump of his fist on the outside, booming. And silence.

Made it, jack! Shit! They breathed, looked at each other. Calliope closed her eyes and let out a big puff of air. Spit wanted to giggle. But then another twist of fear. The lift wasn't moving. He stared at the doors, certain that they were going to open and let the Kaiser in. But then it was okay. There was a lurch, a shudder and the lift started to drop.

"Shit!" Calliope was at the floor buttons, pressing them frantically. "Shit! Shit! Shit!"

"What's wrong, jack?"

"I pressed for up. Floor eleven."

The lift was still falling. Not fast, but down through 3 and 2 and 1 and B and it was still going. The indicator stuck on B as if they were dropping into one big, empty hole and kept on down.

It stopped, though. It had to. Quick, with a shudder. The doors opened. They looked out into an empty concrete lobby lit by a dim yellow light. Spit knew this sort of scene. He'd been here with Blyss to see the Queen of Heaven. And Livid was safe, wasn't he? It was safe down here. He wasn't sure. Calliope pressed at the buttons again but nothing happened. They could hear, in the silence, the whine of the motor in the other lift. It was coming down.

"Come on!" Calliope shouted suddenly and leapt for the outside.

"No, jack! Wait!" Spit reaching out to grab her, missed and it was too late, doors were closing. He got his foot in there but they didn't release, just squeezed. Calliope yelling something, trying to come back, her fingers scrabbling through the gap in the door. Then the lights went out. Calliope screamed.

◊

Ratman playing with the flow. Get all the little protocols and unentangle. Easy-peasy, pritsy-witsy. This was fun. Like juggling. Couldn't stop the stuff but watching it, translating, bursts of bits like colour. Dit, dit, dit and dot, dot, dot. Like a chunk of a vid phone message.

– …o you don't.

What does that mean? Somebody mad, maybe. Practice, Ratman. Got to practice more and get this sorted. Go, go, go and fun, fun, fun.

A green ball burst, exploding in a splash of dirty white and…

– Hi there, sugar.

– What? Who that?

Was scary now. Was something in amongst it. Where? Where, and scare, and there. Could go. No, no. The Queen says stay.

And there it was again, was bigger now.

– WELL, HI THERE, SUGAR. SUGAR MINE.

A swelling bladder, wallow. It was full, the Ratman saw, with words like creatures bathed in brightness, crawling in the bag of it. And a laugh, a kind of laugh.

Oh, no, boy. No!

– Abort! Hey, chip! Abort!

And gone. The darkness crashing in, a lurch, and Ratman's brain like a rolling boulder.

Eyes. Open. Visor up and back in the room then. Blurry lights around the ceiling. Blinked. Oh, boy. The lungs all going hard. The heart. Oh, Cool Eyes. Have to do this thing for you? You do not know.

◇

Blyss called at four-thirty, came onto her screen with that big, loopy grin.

"Ah, Mr Blyss," she said. "So nice of you to respond so quickly."

"How could I not, dear lady. Your invitation was almost peremptory."

She laughed, her most delicate laugh, which she was using now to cover up a sudden surge of anger. She could sense, though, that neither anger nor flirtation would go far with Blyss. That bird-like quality, cold blue eyes. He would have to be out-thought, as charmingly as possible.

"I wanted to attract your attention," she said.

"You did that without a doubt. My poor companion was thoroughly disconcerted. I don't think you did his hypertension any good at all." His grin widened. The tips of his teeth were just visible on his lower lip. "Now, how can I be of help?" he asked.

"Well," she said. "I have a client. Galen Corporation. Or more particularly, Galen Laboratories."

"That must be a lucrative connection for you. Most valuable I'd say."

"As you're probably aware, my professional responsibility is to ensure that the public image of any of my clients is all that it should be. This job, of course, is not made easier with the occurrence of inexplicable events of a very serious nature."

"You mean violence in public places?"

"I mean the failure of certain items of medical equipment."

"I can assure you I know nothing about..."

She interrupted him. "Mr Blyss, please. Unless we are open and honest with each other we shall never get anywhere."

"Hmmm. What do you suggest?"

"I think we should have a little chat. Face to face."

"Well, yes. Why not? That would be absolutely delightful."

"Tomorrow?" she said. "I have somewhere discreet where we could perhaps link in to your associates if necessary."

"My associates?"

"Mr Livid, perhaps."

"Name the time and place, dear lady."

17

Tuck Inn Pie

($1)

Meal of the Moment

All Natural

INGREDIENTS

Reconstituted Protein 779314

Synthetic Cereal CS84938290

SAFWICK Recycled Fibre (biodegradable)

Flavouring: SF34A9, ISF9241

Colouring: PC34-567, PQ959-237

Preservatives: ISP9914, ISP7621

Passed by the Port Nicholson Health Authority

Packet label

Morning, it had to be morning. He knew it somehow, jack. The same little room with the carpet hangings, the pile of cushions, the same little table with the wristic brass pot. The same big vid screen only now it didn't show Livid's face but a movie; images, huge figures, faces looming to the ceiling. Black and white like the old-time geri shit, except that it starred the Queen of Heaven. It was about some young dud trying to be a writer and sucked in deep by this rich slink in a busted mansion. The Queen of Heaven's big moon face filled the wall. She had painted lips in little bows and was sucking on a cigarette in a wristic fucking holder that hooked onto her finger. A movie star, jack, an old star from the silent movies, except the studios had dropped her, dumped her. Well, shit, jack, she was a geri and useless, what did she expect? She'd had her turn.

Spit closed his eyes and tried not to watch. The movies had been going on for hours, like they'd drown out everything and for a while he'd let them. Didn't want to think about it, jack. Didn't want to remember how those lift doors opened and Calliope was gone and there was a butcher he'd never seen before with a shooter, who marched him down the corridors and parked him here. He couldn't fig the worst of it, jack. What was the worst? The shooter pointing at his back? The sound of the turning lock and knowing he was stuck in here? Or wondering how it all fitted, if Kaiser and his butcher sib were tied up with Blyss somehow and that meant with Livid and that meant... Shit, jack, better just to watch the movies.

Except that now it was getting harder, he was vomit with it. He'd sat through the one where the Queen of Heaven like a fat whale, swelling in a swimsuit, was kissed on the beach by some wristic turb while the waves broke over them. And another one where she was a hooker and this rich dud fell in love with her and bought her all these clothes. He turned over, hid his head in the pillows. Couldn't get away. The fat slink, all that puking flesh and lolloping in wrinkled flabs. He was sick. She made him sick. And she had him, jack. She had him on the inside like she had that writer. Scared and hungry and wanting something, all that sick excitement like the first time, laughing as the blood oozed out around her fingernails. The face seemed burnt into his brain. It was looking at him all the time. And the voice talking to him.

"Arlen! Arlen, my little one. You're not paying attention, are you? You're not absorbing your culture, your lovely lessons."

Shit, jack, it was real this time. He lifted the pillow from his head and looked up, slowly. The movie had stopped and

Livid was gazing at him. The Queen of Heaven face, the same, jack, but with a black moustache now and a wristic silver earring in his right ear. Sitting in his wheelchair, all the techno-shit around him, screens and monitors flickering like crazies on the loose.

"Don't you like it?" Livid asked.

"Sure, jack." Playing it safe.

"Have you had enough, maybe?"

"For a little while."

"That's all right. That's quite all right. I want to talk to you anyway. You can find out what happens to Norma Desmond later. Now, tell me if you like working for me."

"Sure, I do." And this is working, jack?

"What do you like about it?"

"A paying job, jack. I never had a paying job."

"Money? How ridiculous! How crass!" Livid laughed and showed a mass of black stumps where his teeth should be. "Money is silly. Money's useless. I can have all the money in the world, you know that? And what good would it do me? No, no, my pet. The main thing is to fulfil your inner potential. Follow your destiny."

Sure, Spit thought. He knew that. It was the ASP philosophy. Was Livid an ASP?

"In the old days," Livid went on, "when I was the White Rabbit, when I was locked up in that silly video game, all I wanted was to have fun. And fun to me then was beating all those other little idiots who came along to try their luck. And when they opened it up to the network so that it all became the one big game of Street Kings and they allowed you to play for real credits, I was free to go where I wanted and I won thousands, ten thousand in a week once, but it wasn't the money that mattered. The money just went to prove I was the best, and that made me feel good. It was wonderful to know how I'd done them in, how they all thought they could take on that silly looking rabbit with their macho-muscled fighters and their kick-boxing heroes, but to no avail, oh no. Their pathetic little egos, their life savings they were trying to parley up into something they could buy a future with, the White Rabbit took it all and rubbed their faces in the dirt. Ha! Ha!" He threw back his head and laughed again, his body trembling, shaking like a huge blancmange. "And the beauty of it was, I didn't want their money. I didn't care about their money. I couldn't even use it. I just wanted the fun of having them know what it felt like when I downed them. And that's why I gave it up really." He was suddenly gone serious, thinking, staring at a point about two meters above Spit's head.

"Why?" Spit asked, because he felt he had to.

"I couldn't see their faces," Livid said. "They never showed me their faces. Now of course it would be different. Now I have the technology and I can see everywhere. Well, not quite everywhere but many, many places and I can see into people's eyes and I can read their thoughts and I can enjoy that special moment when they know, when they realise that I have them, that I've won, that I can subject them to any humiliation I choose. That's fun, don't you think?"

"Sure," Spit said. It was fun, maybe. He felt a twitch of it, a throb of power in his guts. He wasn't into sadis, jack, he wasn't one of those sick wristers who liked to nasty people, but there was a buzz in thinking about it sometimes.

"What you must learn," Livid said, "what you must see is that ideas are the most important thing there is. The eighteenth century philosophers had it right, you see. Only nobody took any notice then because they didn't realise how the physical world can be moulded to the ideal, how technology can transform reality so that information is the only thing that matters. Everything else is just a kind of putty that we push around into the shapes we want. You understand?"

"Sure, jack," Spit said and he maybe did.

"Well, it's all nonsense, so don't take any notice. Philosophy is boring. The real thing is to enjoy yourself, fulfil your inner destiny. You know how to do that?"

"No."

"You need to get in touch with your secret pleasure, your

deep down daring, the pleasure that you're most scared of. There's always such a pleasure, isn't there?"

"Yes," Spit said. He knew that this was true.

"Well, I'm going to help you do that, aren't I? Because I know what your secret pleasure is. Don't worry. I'm not going to give it away. I'm not going to tell you. That would really spoil everything."

◊

"Good morning, Wilfred. I trust you're well." She took the food jar down from the windowsill, fed him one of the little insect nuggets. "A special treat today," she said. "A special day." And it would be, wouldn't it? The dawn sky was a fine orange, pink, purple. Wasn't that supposed to augur well? Because if you were clear about what needed to be done and knew you could do it, everything else fell away into insignificance.

She dropped a second nugget into the outstretched leaves, watched as they closed so smoothly, silently. A real fly would be buzzing in there, helpless. Attracted to the sweetness and suddenly realising, oops, it was trapped and then the panic would set in, if a fly felt any panic, as it began to realise it was going to die.

Well, she thought, I have my own trap to set today. Even if I'm not quite sure who or what I'm catching. She felt relaxed. She felt confident, happy almost. Strange, really. From the moment she had seen the connection between Derek Mountain and what had happened to Cynthia, she had known that nothing else mattered but revenge. It didn't matter who the opposition was or how powerful they were. It didn't matter that she might be taking on the entire strength of Galen Corporation or half the rings in the city's underworld. She felt she could do it. She felt she had the strength and the will and the cleverness.

"After all," she told Wilfred. "You have to put family first, don't you?" And afterwards? Well, afterwards was entirely another thing. Afterwards, if there was such a thing, would almost certainly take care of itself.

◊

Oh boy, oh boy, so what to do? Call Charlie? No. 'Cos maybe Cool Eyes talk to Charlie. Maybe she say stop already. Ratman doesn't want to stop. The Ratman scared now, scared of Froggy, all that big stuff coming in. Froggy fry the Ratman's brain for sure. No, no. Oh boy, oh boy, oh boy, oh boy, oh boy. The Ratman got the shakes now, hands all shaky, legs all go, go, go. It doesn't want to. Doesn't want to fight. So smile, Cool Eyes, smile and let the Ratman free. So let it play and work and play and let it be. And what happens, then, though? No more smiles. No more eyes. And even if the job done well and Froggy dead then no more eyes. So either way the Ratman done for. Either way the Ratman see the Queen no more. So fight, Ratman, fight.

Need a something, though. Need a thought, to kill the code. Froggy just a program. Froggy just a skein of logic, just a clever, clever. Get him maybe. Get inside and see the logic, cut the cord. Yes, yes. The roly-poly. Get that stuff that Ramesh sent and take a look at it. See how a little froggy, simple froggy works and see. For simple is as simple does and code that cuts that little roller maybe cuts off Froggy's head.

18

Saigo Devastated!

How cheap is love? Flint-hearted Fee has dumped her blond big-boy Saigo Bruce ending all speculation about the Romance of the Century. 'It's definitely over,' a tearful Saigo told our reporter. 'It's Fiona's choice and I have to respect that.' Yet another case of the Rich and Fabulous playing fast and loose with the affections of mere mortals? And did Daddy have a hand in it? Last seen, Fantastic Fee, as gorgeous as ever, was consoling herself with a few drinks at Candy's in the company of RAVE star Brad Dunnery. Such Courage in her Suffering!

Pump Trend

The movies, all that wristic shit, were on. They were always on. They never stopped. He couldn't tell the difference any more. He didn't watch. He shut his eyes. But then, after a while, he couldn't help it and opened them again and was there looking like a pissdick droppo or fudge freak, plugged into the wall vid, staring. The same scenes, the same blat over and over, with the Queen of Heaven in a wristic palace somewhere, slaves all dropping to their knees in worship. Or she took baths in milk or massages with handsome duds in loincloths stroking her so her white flesh quivered and her lips were fat with sighs. Or she was stuffing herself, her hands in bowls of food and mouth down into it and grunting like a pig and laughing with the juice and the cream and the gravy, jack, all running down her face. Spit was hungry. He had to watch the food. He couldn't stop himself.

He hated the fat cunt. Right up max, he hated her and no shit SKB. She could do anything. She had all the power but all she cared about was stuffing her huge fat face. It was the size of her that did him, jack. She was like a white wave or cloud that carried him up and he was floating. She could blow him away in a second, leave him falling, done to mush. And she showed him, jack, left him knowing, that an ASP was not enough, that his secret, his only source of power, was like a bubble, a nothing, like a chicken leg in one of her feasts that she could rip the flesh off with her rotten teeth and laugh as her piggy eyes stared down at him, stared at him deep down. Everything she saw, and she could slam him in an instant with one flick of her fat ringed fingers. He watched her and hated her and was scared because he couldn't stop himself.

When he looked at Livid now, he saw the same face, the same look in the turbo piggy eyes. Livid didn't eat. He talked, jack. He coughed the snot. Dressed in his pirate gear, or his bikoe suit, or like a cowboy, jack, with hat and waistcoat with a sheriff's star, he sat in his wheelchair and blabbed at Spit about his destiny. And Livid's destiny was taking over, grabbing information and using it to do some deal or jam some wristers in the deals they tried to do. He had a hundred slammy scams and talked about a new one every minute. Like he was buying computer gear by digging data straight into the ordering system of a buster corporation, paying for it with a credit hook to some other duds who didn't know who or why or when they were being done. He was a slick wrister, cunning. He could do anything he wanted right there from his junk-filled room. He had tapped into the Colosseum security systems and was watching the whole pissdick building, jack, like every corridor and every video call, so much he had a box rigged up to keep track of it, his own slice of space on the security database.

"Use the enemy to watch the enemy," he said. "Some Roman general must have said that."

"That's a slick system, jack."

"All my own work."

"Maybe you could use it to order me some pizza," Spit said.

"Are you hungry? Hell, you can't be hungry. I've only just fed you."

"Or a Colosseum burger, I could do one of those."

"But what about the soul, my friend? The food for your passions?"

"Later maybe."

"Ha! I don't believe you. I don't believe that a young man of your spiritual calibre could be so shallow. I tell you what. I'll prove it to you. I'll prove to you that the hot world of your desires is more important than your stomach. What do you say?"

"Okay. Then can I have a pizza, jack?"

"Without a doubt. Now, let's begin." Livid's face, large in the wall, was beaming at him. Eyes big and glistening like a crazy so you couldn't look at them. "Now, you remember the Queen of Heaven the first time you saw her? And at other times, too, when she's not eating or indulging in her sensate focusing? What does she do?"

The nails on the white skin, the scream of the victims, wristic fuckin wonderland, and SKB.

"You know what I'm talking about. I can tell by your face," Livid went on. "She hurts people, doesn't she? Now why does she do that?"

"Stuff me, jack."

"You know. You do know. There'll be no pizza till you tell me."

"She likes it."

"Yes! And so do you, don't you? You want to crush your victims, just like that."

Spit didn't answer. Couldn't, jack. There was no yes but there was no no either. Only a freako weird confusion, hot in his blood.

"Ha! Ha!" Livid's finger, pointing, ballooned in the wall in a huge, white blob. "You can't fool me. I know all about your little psychosexual ambitions, the way you'd like to feel how strong you are, how powerful. The power of life and death, that's it, isn't it?"

The twitch of it, like a running rat, a fat, grey flurry.

"Because you're an ASP, aren't you?"

Fuck me, jack! The wrister knows!

"Don't look so surprised. It's perfectly obvious what your fantasies are. I doubt if there's anything about you I don't know, Arlen. Because it's my job to know. Information is the stuff of life. It's more important than blood. You realise that? Blood is just the miserable gruel that keeps the body going. But information? Ah! With information you can be independent of the body. You can be immortal, endlessly renewable. Like I am. And isn't that what your little illusions are all about? Your ASPish notions? Omnipotence in secret, isn't that the idea? Well, I'm here to tell you that nothing needs to be secret. The power you can wield from the cave of your mind is real power. The power of life and death. Let me show you."

Blam. There was a flash and the wall vid filled with a new image. A room. A room the mirror image of Spit's own, with the wristic hangings and the cushions in the corner, the same brass jug. Except that lying there with her face turned away and buried in the pillows was a figure, Calliope. Her spiky dark hair was all over the place and her black dress crumpled. She had no shoes on. One leg was drawn up under her and the other, long, pale and skinny stretched out across the floor. Around the ankle was a black strap with a cord attached to it, snaking over the carpet.

"Here you are," Livid's voice said. "I've brought you your little playmate. Someone you can really have fun with."

Spit stared at the image. It wasn't real, jack. It was a movie, a thing that Livid had dreamt up. Yet another dumb kidoda.

"Now," Livid said. "The equipment. Just look under the cushion to your left."

Spit turned over the red and gold pillow. Underneath it, set in the floor, were three buttons.

"Press the middle one," Livid said.

Spit did it. Calliope's image in the vid gave a jerk and twisted, hands clutching at the thing round her ankle. Her mouth and eyes were open. She was screaming. Fuck, jack! Spit shrank away, slammed back against the wall behind him. As soon as his finger left the button, Calliope collapsed with her hands over her face. Her shoulders twitched. He could see her panting. Then, suddenly, she sat up again and began tugging, pulling at the cord around her ankle, trying to yank it free.

"There," Livid said. "The left button lets you talk. The right button lets you listen. With the middle one you can inflict pain. What more do you need?"

◊

She had no doubt that he would keep the appointment. Sitting there in the intimate little reception room, one of dozens in the Colosseum's Business Centre, she felt confident and excited, infused with a sense of her own being. Almost, she thought, as if she were waiting for a lover. Which was strange because Blyss struck her as being a distinctly asexual creature, one of those people whose talk and manner denied any possibility of intimacy. He was entirely intellectual, she decided, and perhaps, in a sense, that was where her peculiar attraction to him lay.

She looked round the little room, at the soft grey walls and thick carpet, the drapes which had a soft swirling pattern like tie-dyed silk, the glass table and the two plump chairs in black synx. There was a single rose on the table in a tall glass vase and the two-metre wall vid, big enough and yet not too dominant, was playing an abstract pattern which blended tastefully with the drapes. It would do, she thought. It was adequate to the purpose; soft without being cosy, efficient without being cold.

He arrived a minute early - she could have predicted it. A discreet tap on the door. When she opened it, there was one of the Business Centre assistants with Blyss a pace behind. He grinned when he saw her, that big clownish grin. Attractive? How could she have ever thought so for a moment?

"Mr Blyss to see you, Ms Tempest."

"Thank you. Some coffee, perhaps. Coffee, Mr Blyss?"

"My dear lady, yes. Why not indeed?"

He stepped past her into the room, rubbing his hands. Long hands with carefully manicured nails. He was dressed in a navy-blue three-piece suit and a red tie. Black shoes with a gleaming polish.

"Please," she said. "Be seated." She closed the door. "So nice of you to come."

"How could I resist?" He spread his hands.

She smiled, sitting down opposite him, folding her legs to one side, laying her arms along the fat arms of the chair. The deliberateness of the movements increased her confidence.

"How does this room suit you?" she asked.

"More than satisfactory."

He would know, of course, that she was recording everything, audio and visual, and she assumed that he had made similar arrangements for himself.

A pause. She looked at him, smiled. He was staring at her, eyebrows raised, lids blinking slowly over his pale blue eyes, an expression which disconcerted her. I have to get him talking, she thought. I have to get him to trust me.

"So why, precisely, did you keep this appointment, Mr Blyss?" she asked.

"I was intrigued, of course. And then the prospect of such delightful company..."

"You flatter me."

"No indeed. A lady of your undoubted charm. I'd even go so far as to use that word in the plural if it weren't so politically incorrect."

"And, of course, you want to know why."

"Of course."

She shifted in her chair, moving her knees to the right, lifting her hand so it touched the side of her neck below her right ear.

"Let me lay my cards on the table," she said. "I want to work with you."

"Do you indeed?"

"I think we can benefit from each other's talents."

"Hmmm. And what precisely would you say my talents were?" he asked.

"A complete lack of principle."

He laughed. "My dear lady, you seem to know me far too well."

"I know a little, Mr Blyss. I believe I know. And I'm interested in what happened with that medical test at Galen Laboratories. It appears that someone hacked into it."

"What an unhappy occurrence!"

"And it would seem that whoever did it had the assistance of a Galen employee who is now dead."

"Even less happy, wouldn't you say?"

"And I believe that this hack was just one of a great many which have been going on under the smoke-screen of what I can only describe as a plague of puerile practical jokes."

This time he said nothing. And suddenly she could see how it could be done.

"My question," she said, "is precisely why are you doing these things?"

The grin was even bigger and the eyebrows arched even higher than before. He seemed about to burst with the amusement of the game. But Lavendar did not need him to answer. There was only one common thread which linked Biling, Robollo, Derek Mountain, Blyss and Livid. Something to do with technology. Something to do with systems and how they worked. And suddenly she saw quite clearly what the purpose behind it all must be.

"More coffee, Mr Blyss?"

"Thank you, dear lady."

◊

— Hey, chip. This is Ratman.

– This is your neural translator chip here. What is your password?

– Me. The Ratman.
– Hello, Ratman. This is your neural translator control chip here. Your registered abort signal is 'abort'. Do you wish to change it?
– No.
– Acknowledge. Please wait for your entry.

19

Ruin Leads to Suicide!

Tawa Police report the suicide of local businessman Fatsuo Molle. Mr Molle, known as The Mole to close associates, was yesterday found dead in his office in Kapiti Plaza. He had apparently taken a drug overdose. Sources say that Mr Molle had been engaged in a takeover battle with unknown interests in recent weeks and had also been the victim of several cases of computer based fraud. His holding company, Blue Mountain Properties, once valued at over two billion dollars, has passed into receivership with debts of at least 75 million.

Full Financials

It was a pisser, jack, a shitnose. He wanted to talk to her but he couldn't. There was something, something stopped him, like his mind was DTM. He just lay there, sat there, staring at her in the wall vid. And she, not knowing he was watching, did her biz: wandering around or lying on her bed or snuffling with her head in her hands. Sometimes she did things that Spit felt bad about seeing, things you would do if you knew you were by yourself. But still he couldn't take his eyes off her and still he couldn't move. Couldn't talk, couldn't listen, couldn't stop thinking about the third button and what it would do. Sometimes she stared at him, stared through the wall as if she could see him, and sometimes her lips moved like she was saying stuff. He guessed then that she was looking at her own vid and that Livid was talking to her, dropping her his Sha-Ka-Bla, or bouncing around in some wristic ballgown. Having his fun. Doing his secret pleasure.

He had to make it, jack. He had to focus. An ASP was a mover, a thing of power. Except he wasn't an ASP any more. He couldn't be because the wrister Livid knew, and if someone knew your power was gone. Because the power came from freedom and the freedom came from secret will. And he knew he could press the button and make her scream out in pain and he knew that's what Livid wanted and that Livid knew what Spit wanted, or at least Spit guessed he did because Livid knew everything, could see into the centre of your brain. So what the fuck did Spit want, jack? And how could he ever know it was his own?

Calliope was sitting on her bed with her head hanging. She had pale skin, almost white, a kind of milky white. Around her ankle where the black cord was, he could see a red mark, rubbed. Or burnt, maybe. Talk to her, he thought. Say something. All you have to do is push the button and talk. His finger hovered. Freaked, jack. She had him freaked because she wasn't just a movie.

Push. The button pushed back at him. He felt it click.

"Hey," he said.

Calliope's head shot up. She stared at her wall vid, straight at Spit and then she looked around.

"Calliope, hey," he said again. This time she said something but he was too slow on the listen button and he missed it.

Like a video game, he realised, playing the buttons like in Street Kings and that was the idea, that was the thought that Livid had, to be like that. Because it's all a game, jack, as any ASP would tell you.

"Hey, jack. If you want to talk to me, you have to take it slow. I got two modes here and I need to switch." He pushed the listen button but she didn't say anything. Shit, jack, this was sick. He tried again.

"If you want to get so I can hear you, you have to signal me. You have to raise your hand first. Okay?"

Slowly, after a couple of seconds, she raised her hand. He pushed the listen button.

"Who are you?" she said.

"It's me, Spit. They got me too."

She started to speak and then she remembered and raised her hand.

"How come you've got those controls, then?" she asked.

"The fat man gave them to me. Livid. I got three buttons here." Shit, jack, he thought. I shouldn't have told her that.

"What for?" she asked.

"So we can talk. It's a game of his. He likes those games."

"So how does it work?" she asked.

"I've got one button so I can talk and one so I can listen." He stopped, wondering what to say next. Her mouth moved. He knew what the question was without listening. So, jack, what to do? Just CTS. Just cough the fuckin snot.

"The third button's hooked to that thing on your ankle."

"Fuck you!" Again he didn't hear and he didn't need to. Her lips and her face showed him and she turned and strode away, out through the door into another part of her cell, the bathroom bit, trailing the black cord after her.

"I didn't know what it did," he said. "I only pushed it once. Any other time was him. Shit, jack, I wouldn't do it, deliberate, would I?"

He pushed the listen button, held it down, but there was no response. The cord, snaking over the floor, gave a twitch as she moved somewhere out of sight. I could get her, he thought. I could push that button and make her jump, make her listen. No kidoda. That's what Livid would do. He'd push. He'd feel the power and he'd laugh. That's what an ASP would do. But who the fuck was an ASP?

"Look," he said. "You and me. We're the only chance we got to get out of here, jack. You hear me?"

◊

Blyss sipped his coffee delicately, his little finger raised in a fastidious gesture like a dowager duchess. "My problem, dear lady, is that I'm not entirely sure of the advantages of using you, if I can be permitted so crude an expression. Your talents are manifest and manifold, of course. Anyone can see. I lead such a simple life, however. My needs (and I mean this strictly in the business sense) are small."

"But your deeds are large," she answered.

"Deeds? You make it sound almost heroic."

"I could have said 'crimes'."

"Whatever do you mean?"

"Production and trade in pornographic materials, industrial espionage, murder perhaps."

"Murder? Good Heavens!"

"Somebody killed Frank Biling."

"Organ snatchers, surely."

"Mr Blyss, please. I can't believe that, if only because my company is the origin of the rumour."

Blyss laughed. "Your company? Delightful."

"I'm not sure entirely why Frank Biling was killed but it was almost certainly because of his association with you. That association, given your connections, could have been a distinct embarrassment to my client. We needed a diversion, therefore."

"So organ snatchers."

"Yes."

"Inspired!"

"It illustrates, perhaps, what I have to offer."

"Hmm," he said, considering. "How much do you really know, I wonder? What do you really think our aims and objectives are?"

"I think you're trying to take over this city," she said. "And if you are, then I want to be on your side." Blyss glanced at her quickly for a moment and then turned away, licked his lips, once, twice. So close now.

"Perhaps it's time I introduced you to Mr Livid."

"Perhaps it is."

He reached into his pocket and pulled out a slim vid remote, clicked a couple of buttons. The image on the wall vid flicked and a large window opened, a room like a study or library, floor to ceiling shelves of books and a handsome pedestal desk. There was a big brown leather armchair with an antique standard lamp behind it and a small table to one side. And a man in the armchair. He was fat and pale, white, with wavy brown hair parted in the middle and he was wearing a brocade smoking jacket and a silk cravat.

"David," Blyss said. "This is Ms Tempest."

"Delighted," Livid replied with lips that curled into a delicate sneer, a sneer that reminded her of something. And she knew instantly that this was the one. This was the person she hated more than any other in the world.

"Frickstone," Livid said. "I believe you're in love."

◊

So, Calliope was slipping him, jack. Ever since she'd come out of the back room she'd ignored him. Just lying there, not talking, not looking at him. A scum deal, in Spit's view, especially when they were supposed to be a two-team and getting the fuck out of here. Almost he wished she'd stayed where she was, out of sight. At least that way he wouldn't have to look at her looking miserable. It wasn't his fault for shit's sake. He didn't mean to zap her. Yes, he did though. Half he did. Hell, jack, how could he do that? All that ASP shit.

"You like music?" he said, just to say something. "What you like? You into the Killer Sound? Paula Flesch? Harry Carey? Me, I don't go for that shit much. Unhealthy, you know? Bad for you, jack."

No response, just lying there.

"And I see on TV the other day how they got these super vegies. BioWonder, they called. Genetic engineering freako. They reck they can grow them in four days and they're fatter than normal. Five out of ten people couldn't taste the difference. And three more thought..."

Blam. The wall was suddenly filled with the big white moon of Livid's face, the mad eyes, the black leather cap on his head.

"Boo!" he said and kept his lips out like he was making a kiss, jack. Freak. The lips like big red wrinkled rubber tubes. "I caught you, didn't I? You're not doing as you were told. You're not having fun."

"I'm having fun, jack."

"I haven't had any indications on any of my equipment that your little playmate has suffered any discomfort whatsoever. She's ignoring you. How can you bring her to heel without discipline?"

"It's not my game, jack. Torture and stuff."

"Oh, come now." Livid's lips smiled wide and twisted like he knew who was scamming who. "We both know how you are. We both know how we all are, don't we? The nature of human beings. Unless we plumb the depths of our depravity, how can we possibly achieve nirvana? Don't let's get all moral, please. That would be *so* boring."

"I fig you've got to find out who you are another way."

"You silly little boy! There is no other way! Unless you pass through hell, there is no paradise, no authenticity. You, an ASP, should know that. Please, please, don't disappoint me. I don't want to have to do all the work myself."

There was a noise from somewhere, a signal from some gear, maybe. Livid's face shrank in the wall. He twisted in his wheelchair and looked at all the technostuff on the far side of the room. Something there. Something called to him.

"I have to go," he said. "I've got fun of my own to attend to. Now don't you disappoint me."

Blink. The wall showed back into Calliope's room. She was standing there, staring at a point above his head.

"Livid," he said. "You see him."

"Her."

"What she say?"

"That I'm a slave in her castle and I have to submit to her pleasure so I can be free."

"Fucking bullshit!"

"Crap, jack," she said.

"Look. We gotta move. We gotta go."

"How?"

"Put your ear up against the vid wall. I'm gonna tap on it. See if you can hear."

She moved close to the screen, pressed her ear against it. Spit grabbed the big brass pot and took it over to her. Shit, jack, she looked freak, just standing there with her ear out. He tapped the pot against the picture of her head. She jumped back. Yes. He could see her mouth making the word.

He leapt back to the buttons. "You just next door," he said.

"How do we get through? Smash the screen down?"

"No. Wait." He thought about it. Had to fig it, jack. If they smashed things down, the butchers would be after them. Kaiser, maybe, or some other turbo dud. "We gotta get that thing off your leg first," he said. "Look, you get your own pot, that brass thing, and you wham it on the floor and wham it and wham it and maybe it split, jack, and maybe then you got a sharp edge you can cut."

She was into it already, had the pot and was bashing it and bashing it. After six or so hits, the handle came off so she grabbed it by the spout and bashed it again and then the spout came off. But by then the bottom was splitting away and shit, jack, she had it, a round thing like a wheel with a jagged edge.

"That's it, jack! You gottim. Now cut the cord. Near your leg. Near as..."

"Won't I get a shock?"

"Not if it's safety cord. That stuff can't short unless it's turned on."

"And if it's not?"

"I dunno, jack."

"Oh, fuck it!" And she was away, sawing at the black cord with the rough edge of the disc. Cutting, he could see it, jack but slow. After a while, her hand got sore so she had to wrap the disc up in some stuff she ripped off the pillow and back to the cutting. Her arm going whip-whap and her head bouncing up and down. It was tough, jack and she had skinny arms and he was freaked she would get a shock or else she'd drop it, jack, like she didn't have the turbs. And then she had it, done!

She looked up at him and waved the loose end of the cord. And her mouth shaping noises. He pressed the listen button.

"Yey! Yey!" She was yelling.

"Got it. We're a two-team!"

"Bet your booties, jack!"

Her hand was bleeding, red snake on her white arm.

◊

The fat man sat smiling. His fat white fingers drummed little rhythms on the arms of his chair, fingers covered in chunky rings. It was an act, Lavendar could tell, a pose, as if his disgusting corpulence were merely a cover for something else. He was gross but he was clever, cleverer by far than Blyss.

"Let me explain how it all works," Livid said. "Frickstone and I have a unique relationship based on a common philosophy. We have a simple view of life. We see it essentially as a game. Winner takes all. Would that be true, Frick?"

"Oh, absolutely, David."

"We're a partnership, you see. An ideal partnership, perhaps. Frickstone is in the world but not of it and I'm of the world but not in it. He acts but I am. I despise the notion of physicality whereas he enjoys the arbitrariness of flesh and blood. This is a combination which gives us... well... Not to put too fine a point on it, it gives us a god-like quality. Immanent and transcendent both. You see what I mean?"

Yes, she could see; the thin man manipulating people, working with the likes of Spotty Face and Frank Biling, while the fat man was doing things inside the systems, interfering, corrupting Cynthia. Because it was a gross and disgusting parody of his own repulsive face that had taken over her sister's image and defiled her precious moment. And it was the fat man who had got into Derek Mountain's head and driven him crazy.

"So," she said, "you deliberately sabotaged that test?"

"Ah, my dear," Livid smiled. "You don't appreciate our subtlety, our efficiency. No. Our excursion at Galen had several purposes. One was to see if we could obtain information from that poor boy. That, I'm sorry to say, was not successful. The more important motive, though was t-t-t-t-t-t-t-t..." His image in the wall vid stuttered, flickered. For a moment she got a strange impression that he was wearing not a smoking jacket but a pink lace ball gown and a flowing blond wig. "To impress our other targets," he said, recovering.

"Targets?" she asked.

"It was a demonstration," Blyss said.

"It's all according to our methodology, you see."

"Do it once and do it right."

"There are three phases," Livid said. "The first is Investigation…"

"…where we gather all the data about our potential targets and their organisations. People like Frank Biling help us with that."

"Then comes Demonstration…"

"…where we show the targets exactly what we can do."

"And finally there is full control."

"Which we generally find falls out quickly and inevitably from a good demonstration."

Blackmail, she thought. For power and for information. "So who was the target in this case? Carl Robollo? Dougall Myerson?"

"Mr Robollo has a vast amount of useful knowledge in the design of certain types of system."

"And Frank, too." Blyss added. "Frank wasn't always a lowly lab technician, you know."

She remembered Knoware Application Design and the fact that Livid had been listed as a shareholder. "You bought into his company. To get his patents?"

"Poor Frank still thought he had a chance to recover his fortunes," Blyss said. "He didn't realise how impossible that was going to be."

"And now you're putting pressure on Robollo?"

"Pressure?" Livid looked dismayed. "That's a very ugly word."

"A demonstration, merely," Blyss said.

"Which we are confident will bear fruit. In the fullness of time. Wouldn't you say, David?"

"Undoubtedly, Frick. We generally find that our little shows are thoroughly convincing, don't we?"

"Yes, indeed, David. Yes, indeed." Blyss was staring at her, grinning, eyes round, cheeks puffed out as if he was going to burst with the amusement of it all. Slowly, without taking his gaze from her face, he lifted the video remote and clicked it.

In the vid wall next to Livid's image a window opened. A woman, old, she seemed terribly old. She had straggly hair streaked with grey and a lined face, frown lines, crows feet and deep gouges from her nose to the corners of her mouth. Her eyes were dark, sad, her expression weary. An expression that had barely changed in all the years since Lavendar had last seen her.

"Ms Karen Spatch, I'd like you to meet your little sister Lucy," Livid smiled.

"Hello, Karen," the woman in the vid wall said. "I wish I could see you in the flesh but this is only a recording. They promised they'd show it to you, though."

"And a promise is a promise," Livid said.

◊

Ratman waiting. Understood the principles, the Froggy core. But not thinking it, no, no. Keeping the brain open, watching the genflak, all the shear come in. Look at me now, Charlie. Hey, hey, hey. The Ratman doing it, and daring it. The thing they said that never could be done. The brain in a wire.

– So Froggy, where are you?

And true and blue. Like the Queen's blue eyes, her cool eyes, pool eyes. Ratman knows the...

– HELLO, MY DARLING!

There! A big, big, boomer, huge and puffy like a cloud, coming at him out of the dark.

– HOW NICE OF YOU TO VISIT ME! WOULD

YOU LIKE A CUP OF TEA OR WOULD YOU RATHER DO BATTLE!

Thing like a face, a puffy, saggy face, big, dark eyes, like holes.

– Talk, talk, talk. Ratman want to talk.

– TALK? OH, GOODY. OH, GOODY, GOODY, GOODY.

– Who you be?

– ME? I'M THE WHITE RABBIT, KING OF THE NETWORKS. I'M SURE YOU'VE HEARD OF ME.

– No, no.

– SO WHO ARE YOU?

– The Ratman.

– RATMAN?

Face swelled. Up behind, inside, the other things: ideas and images. Ratman kept the brain quiet, looking for the core. Had to get inside. It was twitchy-itchy now.

– So what you be? A construct? Or manifestation?

– PHILOSOPHY? FANTASTIC! I LOVE TO PLAY PHILOSOPHY. WHY DID THE CHICKEN CROSS THE ROAD? ANSWER ME THAT.

– You a random event, maybe.

– GREAT! YOU GOT THAT ONE RIGHT. HERE'S ANOTHER. TO WHAT DEGREE IS REALITY SOCIALLY CONSTRUCTED?

– You a result of network conditions. Spontaneous generation.

– RIGHT AGAIN! RATMAN, YOU REALLY SOMETHING. I HAVEN'T HAD SO MUCH FUN IN MINUTES. NOW, HERE'S NUMBER THREE, FOR THE GRAND PRIZE, A TRIP FOR TWO TO THE WORLD OF FANTASY. WHY ARE WE HERE?

– You a virus. So who did your code, man?

– WRONG! YOU CAN'T ANSWER A QUESTION WITH A QUESTION. YOU CAN HAVE A CONSOLATION PRIZE, THOUGH. TWO HOURS OF MOVIE MAGIC. HOW ABOUT GLEN CLOSE IN *FATAL*

ATTRACTION? OR *CLEOPATRA* WITH ELIZABETH TAYLOR? OR *SAMSON AND DELILAH* WITH GINA LOLLOBRIGIDA AND VICTOR MATURE? I CAN DO BOTH PARTS IF YOU LIKE. NUDE. THE NUDE VERSION.

Face swelled bigger, closer. Eyes like caves. In the left one, lights there, double line of torches, marching, voices. People. Column of soldiers wearing armour, clank of swords, their spears held high. And down, down, down they came. The Ratman waiting.

NOW! The Ratman went for it and up and in and turned it over. Saw how it was and slashed out, bashed out, thinking flak to hack the soldiers.

– BATTLE? IT'S A BATTLE! WHOOPEE, IT'S A BATTLE! And the face heaved, falling in itself, a twisting spiral, tight, down, like a waterspout. And then a white rabbit with floppy ears lined with pink and a pink button nose, and stiff white whiskers.

– BOUNCY! BOUNCY! BOUNCY! KILL! KILL! KILL!

Straight for Ratman. Open up to it and let it come and went straight in there, looking for the little bit, the key. And BANG! Gone. Rabbit gone. The Froggy Rabbit. Nowhere. Just a little voice-like echo.

– CAN'T CATCH ME, YOU SILLY TWIT. BUT I'LL BE BACK. DON'T YOU WORRY.

◊

"What do we do now?" Spit asked.

"I don't know. Smash the wall down. Have you got anything to hit with?"

"Only one of those wristic brass jugs. That might do it."

"No," she said. "What if it doesn't work? We might just break the circuits or something. We'd be worse off. We wouldn't even be able to talk to each other then."

"SKB, jack. A tough buster."

"What we need to do is get someone here. One of the guards."

"You fig they'll just let us out?"

"We could tackle him, the two of us. With the power cord."

"How we get them to come?"

"Make a noise. They must listen, somewhere. They must check on us sometimes. Look!" She wound off the strip of pillow from her cut hand, wiped it all across her neck and face. Still bleeding, jack. The red smears down her cheek across her throat. "I'm going to kill myself!" she screamed. "I can't stand it any more!" Back she fell across the bed, all twisted up. Blood mess over her face.

Spit took the hint.

"Hey!" he yelled. "She's mushed herself. The sister mushed herself. Where the fuck are you bastards, jack?"

◊

"Well, bless my soul! Would you look at that! Isn't that truly astonishing!" Blyss staring at the wall vid. Instead of the images of Lucy Spatch and Livid in his study there were dozens of windows opened up, all with scenes of confusion: battlefields, crowds, explosions, storms.

"I want them back here," Lavendar said. "I want them both back here."

"I'm not really sure that..."

"Aren't you people in control of these things?"

"Control? In control?" And he started to laugh, throwing his head back and then forward, doubling over, clutching his stomach like a man in pain.

She stared at him, despising him, but frightened too. Frightened for herself in all this chaos, chaos in her heart as much as on the screen before her.

Blyss was staring at her, eyes huge, tears streaming down his face like a weeping man. He was sobbing.

"I won't let you," she said. "I just won't let you." Then she yelled at him. "Do you hear me?"

That got to him, but only just. Shaking his head, wiping his eyes.

"How wonderful, how wonderful," he said.

"You don't care, do you?"

"Care?"

"You don't care about anything."

"Care about?" he stared at her, confused. "Well, care about. Well, care. What does care mean? Is there anything important to me? Yes, I imagine so. Although I can't think what at the moment."

"If you don't care, how do you do anything? How do you act?"

"With difficulty." Serious, just for a moment. Nothing of a grin. And the seriousness was an edge she had, an advantage.

"I need something to set me off," he went on. "Some stimulus. It might be anything. And then once it's moving, it moves. It has its own momentum."

"You don't know who you are."

"Oh, but I do, I do. Don't say that." The look of hurt came back for a moment. "Livid says that. He talks endlessly about authenticity. But he knows nothing about it. And neither do you. I'm the one who laughs. I'm the one who sees the joke in it all, aren't I?"

There was a swordfight going on on the wall. A muscular, bare-chested hero with a bandanna tied round his head was flashing blades with a pirate on the deck of a ship. Then, suddenly, Livid was back, sitting in his armchair as before, except that his cravat was rumpled and his hair, a wig, was askew.

Blyss doubled over, laughing once again.

"Sorry about that," Livid said, patting at the wig, pushing it further to one side.

Blyss laughed even louder.

"Where were we?" Livid asked. "Ah, your little sister."

"You won't beat me," she said. "You won't control me. Not that way. Not any way." A panic deep down in her, wondering if it were true; because how could she live if everybody knew.

"Don't be ridiculous," Livid said. "Frick and I are God. Remember? Well, we must be, mustn't we? I don't see anyone else volunteering for the job. And we have the power. See. Look." The vid split and the left-hand side began flickering with images, on and off, showing places and people, noise and conversation, a rush of actions impossible to distinguish. "We have everyone, everyone here. And we can do what we like with them. Anything at all."

"You're nothing," she said. "You don't exist."

"Exist? Of course I exist. I think, therefore I am."

"You're a figment, an accident."

"At this very moment I am taking over. All these people, all these systems. Even as we speak, I am addressing the people." He gestured towards the rows of images. Suddenly, they were all replaced by a picture of Livid himself wearing a dark suit with a red tie and matching handkerchief in the breast pocket. "Even as we speak this magnificent vision of calm authority is appearing on every TV and every computer screen in the city."

"Ladies and Gentlemen," the image said. "Be calm please. There is nothing to be afraid of. No cause for alarm. I am merely here to announce the new order, the new dispensation…"

"Stop him!" she said, turning to Blyss.

"Good Lord, no. Why on earth should I do that?" And he was laughing again.

◊

Ratman hurt. Ratman pain. Not the body but the brain. The logic, couldn't get it straight. Oh, Charlie, Charlie, Ratman not be good no more. And Cool Eyes, oh.

It was waiting now. Wait. Wait for the Froggy Rabbit. Had to get it this time. One more shot. Couldn't get inside it, not that way. Had to take it in, instead, like a packet on the night fix. Had to open up to it and get the head around it. Had to. Kill you, Ratman. Too late now, though. Should've thought.

Silence. Darkness. Tick, tick, tick. And click, click, click. The Ratman has to understand.

And it was there. The rabbit, big, with tiger fangs and claws like swords.

– I HAVE YOU STUPID! KILL! KILL! KILL!

And Ratman didn't go for it this time. Ratman let it come on in, and gobble, gobble. Eat you Froggy. Ratman like a big, dark, hunger cave, the whole lot, every little, am your brain Froggy. Ratman am your evil brain.

– Hey Froggy me.

– I'M A SILLY ONE, A SILLY ONE, A SILLY, SILLY ONE.

– We friends, Froggy.

Froggy rolling, taking over. Ratman lets him come and doesn't think. It's just a bunch of lines of code, a thing to get the brain around, and watch it, watch for where the key is. Not the Rabbit's head, no, no. It's fluffy, puffy body-o.

So now!

The Ratman switches modes and see the tangle, all that logic, see the main line clickety click. The piece there, how it all fits in, the heart of it, the little knot of logic, randomness. The F. For Froggy. Little change to it, the flick, to turn it off.

The rabbit screamed.

It was gone.

◊

The lights were out. In the dark, jack. The wristic, fuckin dark. But then the wall slammed on with Livid's room and him, the fat freak, in his wheelchair bowling, bowling up and down. He was moaning, jack, like someone mushed him.

Spit pressed the button to talk to Calliope. "Hey, Cal, howzit go?"

"Sweet, jack. I got the Princess on the wall here. She's in bed. Looks like a death scene."

"Stick to the scam, jack. Stick to the scam."

Zoom! The fat freak was coming in.

"Who you talking to, Arlen?" The wall big face. There was blood oozing from beneath the corners of his eyes. "They hurt me, Arlen. They hurt me. No need to hurt poor Livid, was there? Just a little fun. It was fun. I was only having fun." He was mumbling, chewing up his words, jack. Lots of blood on his slack lips now. "You should help me. You should help me get them, Arlen."

"You gotta help Cal first. She done herself."

"I don't care about her. I don't want to know. I'm more important than any of your stupid stuff. Think what the world will lose, what a wonderful phenomenon, if anything should happen to me."

"Get some help, jack. Push the button."

"Absolutely not. That filthy little slut!"

"Fuck you, jack!" Spit with the brass pot, swinging it, flying at the wall. Livid screamed. A smack as the thing hit the glass. The vid went blank.

Spit on the talk button. "You there?"

"Yes."

"Can't see you, jack. That wrister pulled the plug."

"I guess... Wait! Someone's coming!"

"Yell me when you want it!"

Waiting, listening.

"Shit!" said a voice, a man's voice, big, and then feet across the floor. Waiting. Then she screamed. Spit hit the middle button, slam in the juice, jack. Held it. Couldn't tell. Couldn't hear. Couldn't see. He counted five and then he let go, pressed listen again. Nothing, jack. Silence. He tried speak.

"You okay?"

Nothing. Blown it. Juiced the two of them. A double fry. So shit, jack. Shit, oh, shit.

Then a noise. The door opening. Cal was standing there. Staring.

"Hi," she said. "Is that you?"

"Who else, jack?" He stood up. "Me and only. We better move."

"Sure." She turned, going like zip. He was after her.

◊

When the lights came on again the wall vid was going crazy. The right half was flickering with images of Livid, sometimes in a suit, sometimes in the smoking jacket and cravat. The left-hand side was scattered with shots from dozens of security cameras, chaotic scenes of people milling in corridors, stuck in lifts, and traffic jams in the streets outside.

Blyss, curled up in his chair, was whimpering with laughter.

"Frickstone!" Livid was saying. "Frick, dear Frick. Oh, please!"

"Oh no, oh no, oh no." Blyss moaning, with tears streaming down his reddened cheeks.

"Please, dear Frick. I'm hurt. They've done something. It's all coming apart."

"Ha, ha, ha, ha, ha, ha." Blyss's finger pointing at the face in the wall. It was staring at them, fixed, mournful. Blood oozed from the corners of its mouth.

"Look, my friend. Look what they've done to me!"

Lavendar could hardly bear to see but she had to make herself, had to face her horror. "You're nothing," she said. "I can just turn you off."

"Oh, please!"

"I can pull the plug. Flick the switches. That's what you're scared of, isn't it? That all those switches just get turned off."

"Unfair! Horrible, horrible! Unfair!" He was staring at her with big eyes. Crazy eyes. Blyss was crowing with laughter. And suddenly there was only the face of a toy rabbit with one ear horribly mangled, stuffing sprouting from a gaping hole. A whimpering sound, but that might have been Blyss.

And then the screen went blank.

◊

Ratman, Ratman. Where you be?
In the dark. Alive?

Oh, Cool Eyes. Brain hurt.
Let's get out then.
Abort. Hey, chip. Abort.
Nothing.
Nothing coming out of the wall cable. Dead connection.
Sending out a signal hit a burnt-in wall.
Stuck, then. Stuck, stuck, stuck.
So what now? What now Charlie?
Ratman all alone.

20

Sabotage Denied in Network Chaos

Commercial enterprises were left this morning counting the cost of yesterday's major failure in the Southern Information Systems Intracity Network. Not only was the whole city thrown into chaos for over twenty minutes but a number of fail-safe storage and back-up systems were not properly triggered. Most major corporations have reported significant loss of data. Mary Yeadon, Intracity Operations Manager, denied that the failure was the result of sabotage. "The image which appeared on everyone's screen for a few seconds seems to have been a randomly generated phenomenon." Port Nicholson Police, however, are reported to be seeking the whereabouts of Mr David Livid of David Livid Enterprises, whose premises in Johnston Street were destroyed by fire at the time of the disaster.

News in Brief

"Arlen? Is that you?"

The Farter and Muddler at the kitchen table. He stood in the doorway, hovering.

"You haven't been back five minutes and you're off again," the Farter said.

"Don't be hard on the boy, Clive. He's had a tough time."

"He's been gallivanting, playing around. How can he expect to draw his money if he doesn't stick to the district. Fair's fair."

"He's got a job, Clive."

"He had a job! David Livid Enterprises. You saw it on the TV. Up in smoke. Is that a job?"

Spit didn't argue. He didn't have the stuff to argue, jack. He had money in his pocket but shit all else. And when the money ran out?

"I expect he's going to school like a good boy," the Muddler said.

"Is he? Is he going to school?"

"Sure," Spit told him.

"Well, everybody's got to learn. That's your duty, boy. Can't take your money if you don't learn."

"I'm off," Spit said.

◊

Lavendar Tempest sat in her kitchen, not looking her best, not feeling it. A horrible morning. She had hardly slept with the chaos in her mind churning on and on. And she didn't know why really because the thing with Blyss and Livid was all over. There was nothing they could do to her. Even if that videoplay of the Lucy person turned up somewhere nobody was going to believe it was real. It was just some invention, a thing they created to get power over her. And she'd rejected it. She still rejected it. There was no need to go back, was there? Nothing to go back to.

She called into the office, picked up her messages. There were a dozen or more: Gordan Sapich, Mark Bullington, Curtis Caid, a person from the Mayor's office. Madeleine Drummond saying not to worry, everything was all right. Curtis again because he'd been speaking to Carol Carlion about her and Carol seemed really interested. Carl Robollo saying a personal thank you. Eight calls from news reporters. She was a celebrity, it seemed. Just as she'd always wanted to be. The thought of it made her tired.

She dialled up Simon but left the vision off so that he would not have to look at her in this state. He'd dyed his hair again, a soft dark red today. It suited him.

"How are you?" he asked.

"Awful. I don't want to talk to anyone. I feel like a monkey with a hangover," she answered. "And I bet I look like one too."

"Don't worry. Take your time. Look, you want me to handle the media?"

"Please."

"How should I play it?"

"However. The heroine is resting. Something like."

"But you don't want I should close it down. You'll want to pick up on it, take advantage, won't you? Tomorrow, maybe." He was eager, almost pleading. He could sense the opportunity.

"I guess." But she was thinking, who cares? He can do what he likes.

"I'll call you," she said.

"Ciao."

Ciao. And who else had said that? Curtis? Or was it Mark? It seemed years ago, another life. But her own life, wasn't it? The only one she'd got. She remembered the time when she'd first come to Port Nicholson, standing in the entrance floor of the Eliades Complex. Smooth floor of marble, chandeliers above with myriad reflections. Everything good is in a place like this, she had thought. The best people in the finest setting, resplendent. And she had relished the word because it had such a nice sound to it, rich and hopeful. And the glitter of glass was like the assembled brilliance of the city and she could, she knew, be one of those pieces, crystal, in her place.

So what had changed?

She looked at Wilfred with his glossy feeder leaves spread open, waiting, hopeful. Thought about the room where she had confronted Blyss, the image of Livid in the wall. The crazy rabbit with the torn ear. I won, didn't I? she said to herself. I did win.

But then there was that image of the Lucy person, the sister she had left behind. Yes, sister, how could she deny it? A person who was younger than herself but looked thirty or more years older, a person still perhaps living in that way, in that cheap dingy, hopeless, helpless world down on the street. Alone, yes. Lucy would be alone because there was no one else, was there? Never had been, not since they were quite small. My guilty secret, she thought. My awful, guilty secret. And the reason I'm alone myself.

She stood up, looked out of the window, at the city towers in the morning sunlight. Gently, and for the first time in as long as she could remember, she began to weep.

◊

"Hey, buzz, where you bin?" Jank standing, leaning against the wall by the phones.

"Hi, jack."

"You find that card, buzz?"

"No."

"Well, you lucked it, buzz. You hear the glads about them ATMs?"

"No. What happened?"

"They bin eating up cards, buzz. Some catch on fire."

"They burn 'em?"

"Sweet as, buzz. The welfare asking for all the duds have lost a card go down and reregister."

"Bullshit!"

"No bullshit, buzz."

So maybe it was so.

"Anyway, buzz. I see you around."

"Sure, jack. Stay slick."

Jank moved away and Spit stepped up to the phone, dropped a dollar in the slot, dialled a number.

"Hello, Robollo residence."

"Hi, this is Arlen Wilson calling for Miss Calliope Robollo. I'm sorry I can't give you visual, but this is a public phone and it's been vandalised."

"Just one moment, Mr Wilson."

Waiting. Jank was walking away, slowly down the corridor,

little droppo slouch to her shoulders. She didn't look round. Droppos never did.

A voice in his ear. "Jack, is that you?"
"Hi, Cal. How's it going?"
"Great. What you doing?"
"Nothing."
"You want to come down town?"
"Okay."
"Meet you in Selfies."
"Where's that?"
"Colosseum. South East Tower, level sixty two."
"Take me thirty."
"Great."

◊

So Ratman. This the ee-en-dee. Ratman in the hard a dead man. Knows the stuff, though. Knows the roller, all that Froggy, has the whole huge monster in his head and silenced. Cut his cord. The Ratman did it, Cool Eyes. The Ratman bring you Froggy on a plate, and Ratman's head on a plate. You happy now? You should be happy, got the thing you wanted. Ratman can't be there now, nowhere to go. Not knowhere. Because the Ratman's body lying dead in room 95, BG 6, Crossing Tower, 81 Willis. Start to stinking one day soon. And then? Poor Ratman in here all wired up. With a dead Froggy in his head, flip-flop. A flip and flop and hip and hop. Could do it, though. Could go there, look you through the screen into those Cool Eyes, eh? Could see you. Flip and flop and hip and hop, my lady. Bounce, bounce, bounce.